Minimum Competency

Minimum Competency

A novel about education, testing, life, and death in upstate New York

Jim Mortensen

iUniverse, Inc.
New York   Bloomington

Minimum Competency
A novel about education, testing, life, and death in upstate New York

iUniverse books may be ordered through booksellers or by contacting:

iUniverse
1663 Liberty Drive
Bloomington, IN 47403
www.iuniverse.com
1-800-Authors (1-800-288-4677)

ISBN: 978-1-4401-3947-5 (pbk)
ISBN: 978-1-4401-3946-8 (dj)
ISBN: 978-1-4401-3948-2 (ebk)

Printed in the United States of America

iUniverse rev. date: 5/18/2009

Dedication

I would like to dedicate this book to all those teachers, past, present and future, who have, are or will put up with educational mandates, administrative directives, standardized testing requirements and all other types of educational static that interfere with their time to educate students. In spite of all of the above, you have, are or will make it possible for your students to read this book and earn enough of a living so they can afford to buy it.

Acknowledgments

I would like to thank my wife, Karen, and two daughters, Kirsten and Sigrid, for reading through the several versions of this novel and encouraging me to continue with it. Likewise a former colleague and high school English teacher, Joan Swertfager, for reading through and telling me she enjoyed it and it should be published. It helps when someone appreciates your work and sense of humor.

Introduction

This story is set in an area of New York State that, for those who think of New York State and New York City as a single entity, may be surprised to know exists. Rural, poor, conservative, Republican, sparsely inhabited and with a fluctuating population, it is an area that, whether they like it or not, is dependent on the large cities of the state and Downstate (defined as the area from Westchester County south and out onto Long Island) for monetary support. This is especially true for their school systems which simply cannot meet the educational needs of their students by raising revenue from real estate taxes. Kaaterskill Central School is such an institution.

Kaaterskill Central School—or KCS—is a centralized district sitting on the western rim of the Catskill Mountains of New York State. Because of the sparseness of the population the district is both large—20 miles east and west by 28 miles north and south—and poor. Given this size and the fact it covered most of Palatine County, the school district and county are synonymous as both an educational institution and a governmental entity. One is run by an elected board of education, the other by the board of supervisors (all of whom are Republicans) elected from the small towns within the county.

This school district has been created by centralizing a collection of small town schools scattered in the cloves and hollows of the worn down plateau know to the early Dutch settlers as the Kaaterskill Mountains— thus the name of the school. As the population served by these local schools decreased and the old-timer teachers who worked for peanuts opted for retirement, these small town schools could no longer meet a semblance of an education for the money available. Over the cry of "They are taking our identity away from us!" the voters in these smaller districts reluctantly chose to centralize with the surrounding ones. The main influence on the outcome of this vote to centralization came from a huge financial incentive offered by the New York State Education Department. The thinking was that this new, larger district would produce better education at a lower cost and, thus, pay back the State through the savings. Given the economics of the area and the rising cost of education, this was seen as the only way for the locals to finance schooling for their children. Therefore, facing up to reality, the voters passed the resolutions and, after a few years of juggling students between buildings in several of the original schools, a sleek, new, relatively modern, building to house all the district's seven hundred plus junior and senior high students was built in Snyder's Corners.

Snyder's Corners is the only sizable city/town in Palatine County and the county seat. Situated as it is, almost in the dead center of the new school district, it was an ideal location for the newly formed district to place their major building since it meant no student had more than an hour bus ride either to or from school each day. Moreover the finances were right. The Board of Education president's brother owned a sizable piece of land just outside of town and made an offer to the district at a nice profit to himself. Inasmuch as the district had all that bonus money from the state, no one objected to one of their fellow citizens making a nice bit of cash.

Goodness knew, the county was not a rich one. Aside from a few small manufacturing companies—mostly linked to forest products or bluestone quarries—the last major employer left the county years ago first for an area that had better transportation facilities and, later, for a country with a source of cheaper labor. This meant that unless one was in the service trades, willing to commute to a job out of the area, or could find summer employment taking care of tourists, jobs were hit or miss and, primarily, unskilled and seasonal. This caused cyclic spikes in the unemployment numbers, the result of which meant the biggest sources of family income in the region came from food stamps and welfare. This joblessness created a financial crisis for local government and the school district since neither could depend on money collected from local real estate taxes. Given their income, or lack thereof, the tax revenue needed to run both institutions tended to be hit or miss, depending on when, and if, most residents paid their assessed taxes.

There was, however, recent optimism concerning a proposed casino on the Indian reservation located along the northern edge of the county. While this would not mean an increase in property tax, at least it was hoped this casino/resort would create year-round employment and allow some residents to get off the welfare rolls. Unfortunately the tribe was squabbling amongst themselves as to if, when, and how this was to be built and who would control the action. Until such time as this tribal dispute was settled, these jobs were "pie in the sky" as far as the locals were concerned.

Given the lack of local industry and the fact that much of the land in the district was either part of the Catskill State Park, the Indian reservation, or belonged to the New York City Water Department—all of which made it tax exempt—it was hard to raise the needed money to operate either the school or local government. While initially, New York City paid enough to more than make up the taxes lost on the land flooded to create their reservoirs, eventually Gotham City's Fathers came to realize they were being overassessed and, after winning a lengthy court battle, were able to reduce their payments. This resulted in an even smaller tax base which compounded this crisis further. Forced to make up for this reduction, the county fathers had to do a bit of creative assessing, or, more aptly put; "soak the downstaters".

This meant putting the burden on the only reliable source of real estate tax income, nonresidents. Since seasonal residents purchased much of the taxable land in the area to build summer homes and "camps" there seemed no reason why, in the thinking of the county legislators, these people should not pay for the privilege. As a result, the nonresident owners found the assessed evaluation of these country homes exceeded that of their homes in Westchester County, out on Long Island, in Pennsylvania or New Jersey and the real estate taxes were correspondently higher. Given that these owners were not voting residents, the town supervisors had no qualms about sticking it to them and, in truth, this was the most reliable and major source of tax revenue.

However, the county fathers had to walk a tight line here between collection and forcing these "pigeons" out of the county, which placed a limit as to the amount of revenue that could be raised this way. The naked reality of this meant that the primary source of financing for the county government and school had become more and more dependent on the largess of the state government's revenue sharing as well as state and, to a lesser extent, federal aid. This was especially true at KCS where the school board had rapidly depleted the extra funds given to them as incentive for centralization by expanding the athletic facilities so the boys' football and basketball varsity teams could better compete for a state title. The KCS Board of Education felt these athletic programs were especially important to the local residents since, aside from the school's interscholastic athletic program, most had little or no interest in what went on in the school other than that it took their kids off their hands for the day.

More than half of the residents had grown up in the area; the majority having either dropped out of school before graduation or just made the final cut by taking a lot of easy, "local" courses. Largely unemployable—even if jobs were available—these "graduates" tended to marry early, reproduce often—sometimes without regard for whether their spouses were the father/mother of the child—and send their prodigy back to the institution that "educated" them. On the off chance that the combination of DNA produced a child with the brainpower to take actual rigorous courses and get some kind of advanced education, the likelihood was poor that such individuals would remain in the area. This further eroded the intellectual base as well as any possibility that there would be an uptick in the tax revenue.

As if that were not enough, the next largest parental group in the district consisted of relocated downstaters who, because they were afraid of the drug and violence in the "City" schools, migrated into Palatine County. Most simply sold their downstate homes and got out. Taking the cash and their kids, they purchased a piece of land in Palatine County where they could pull in a doublewide or put up a modular home, drill a well, dig a septic system and settle down. Unfortunately, this was done in such haste, that the new residents gave little thought as to how they were going to earn a living once in the area. Consequently, after the money from their home sale ran out and, with the dearth of employment opportunities, most simply joined the ranks of the locals on the welfare and delinquent tax rolls. This caused a division within the county between the new and old residents since the older residence chose to blame the increase in the social service costs entirely on these newcomers.

Additionally, the drug and violence problem that the downstaters tried to escape just came along with them in the form of their own children whose numbers, addictions, and behaviors added to the school district's financial woes. This number increase happened to coincide with the State Educational Department's issuing of mandates concerning the necessity to educate every child, especially with attention to those with addiction and behavioral problems—mandates that were not covered by increased financial aid. Finally, just when things seemed as though they could not get worse, the U.S. Congress enacted President Bush's No Child Left Behind Act which added more unfunded mandates while threatening severe penalties to school districts that failed to achieve these goals.

If one wanted to get a cross-section of the population in Palatine County they had only to look at the KCS Board of Education for a representative sample. There were five members: an out-of-work used car salesman originally from Central Islip on Long Island; the manager of the local convenience store—the Stop 'N Go—who had been assigned to the area by the parent corporation's CEO who was also his brother-in-law; a third generation farmer; a stay-at-home mom; and the owner of the local insurance agency. This latter member was also the president of the board. In other words, you had three locals and two newcomers, one of whom did not live in the county by choice.

Of the five, only the farmer, housewife and insurance man had graduated from the local high school and had some post scholastic education. The farmer had gone for two years to Cobleskill Ag and Tech and graduated with an associate's degree in animal husbandry. He had run for the board in an attempt to reduce real estate taxes, especially on land designated for agricultural use, only to find he was powerless to do so. As a result he became a contrarian, always voting against any kind of project that added to the district's cost and agitating for cost cuts. The housewife had attended two years at the State University of Cortland as an elementary education major until an untimely pregnancy resulted in her dropping out to get married to a man who may, or may not, have been the father of the baby. She was not a stay-at-home mom by choice but because there were no other opportunities for her in the area and she looked upon her involvement on the Board as a career whereby she could put her shortened college training to use. In this capacity she fancied herself to be an advocate for the teachers who, in turn, considered her to be a meddling pain in the ass. The insurance man went to Syracuse University on a partial basketball scholarship only to lose it when he tore his ACL as a redshirt freshman. Subsequently he dropped out and came home to work in his father's insurance agency. Shortly thereafter he inherited the business when his dad drowned while trout fishing the west branch of the Delaware River—a result of the NYC Water Department making an unexpected release from the Cannonsville Reservoir. While the father had been a good businessman in building up the agency, the son was not and lived, primarily, on the residuals from insurance already sold. However, since his father had seen serving on the Board of Education as part of his civic duty—and a good way to sell insurance—the son followed in the tradition. Additionally, as an exjock, he was front and center on anything that meant improvement of KCS's athletic program regardless of cost.

As far as the other two members were concerned, they belonged to the board primarily because they had been pushed into it. The car salesman, because he had a son interested in football, became a member of the school's booster club. He proved to be a valued member because, since he had no employment, he was free to offer a lot of time to the club's activities. As a result he was elected the club's president and, when a seat on the Board of Education became vacant two years ago, was pushed by the club's members to fill it. He ran unopposed so was easily elected despite the fact his son was a senior and soon to graduate. The Stop-N-Go manager also won as an unopposed candidate. He had entered the election only because his brother-in-law strongly suggested it might be a good idea from a business standpoint. Neither of these men cared one way or the other what went on at the school so usually voted with the majority on any decision—assuming they showed up for the meetings.

Given this varied background and lack of interest or knowledge of how to run any kind of business, much less an educational institution with an underfunded budget in excess of ten million dollars, the Board of Education had to rely on the expertise of a district superintendent to keep things operating smoothly. This required a Chief School Officer (CSO) who was adept in both financial and educational matters. Unfortunately, Dr. Everett Shay, the person currently holding this position, was neither.

Chapter 1

It was not a good Monday morning for Moses Barkman. Sunday night's rain had screwed up the reception on his satellite dish and, when that finally cleared, the pay-per-view, no holds barred, smack down, WWE wrestling match he had ordered was partly over. By the time the rerun started, he was almost through the first six-pack of Premium Genesee Beer and, since he could not remember who won or lost the bout, he had to stay up and watch the whole damn thing again on the rerun. This meant consuming a second, and his final, six-pack. Now, the combination of the late night and cheap beer was not making for an especially pleasant morning. To make matters worse, his welfare check had arrived in last Friday's mail and, since it was Monday, it meant it was about time he got to town to cash it. While he could have had the check directly deposited, he was not one to trust any damn bank to handle his money; he wanted the cash in his hands. Besides, a trip to town and the cash would at least give him a chance to restock his supply of Camels, Genny and Slim Jims at the Stop 'N Go.

Moses lived about three miles from the center of Snyder's Corners at the end of a single-lane, dirt road. The area around him was mostly second growth timber that, after having been logged a number of times, had now reached the point where anything that was worth cutting was long gone. Maybe in another hundred years, if there were no major infestations of gypsy moth larvae or other exotic insects, it might merit harvesting again. Not that Moses minded. Since the land had been logged over and was not near any kind of fishable stream or lake, the land was worthless to outsiders that might buy it up for delinquent back real estate taxes. Moses was a prime candidate for this, since he had not paid his real estate taxes—school or county—for five years.

As long as his rural road was not snow-covered—a common factor in the winter months—it normally took five minutes for Moses to drive his Ford pickup to town, including a stop at the mailbox located where this dirt road met New York State Route 618. Today, however, it was going to take a bit longer since deer season was only a couple of weeks away and Moses wanted to check a piece of cover for deer-sign on the way. There was one area in particular that had a small run-down apple orchard next to a shallow pond which made it ideal deer habitat. Moses had considered putting up a tree stand in one of the apple trees assuming there was enough encouraging deer-sign around to make it worthwhile—of course, too, that would have meant that he have to find wood, nails and the ambition to build the stand. Of the three, the latter was decidedly lacking.

So he decided he would just check the cover and, if he found anything, file it away for later use. This examination did create one more problem for him, however, because in order to check the cover thoroughly he would have to park his truck on the shoulder of Route 618 and walk down a deer path for about a hundred yards through overgrown brush and blackberry brambles. This was nothing Moses was especially fond of doing on even a good day much less one when he was still feeling the effects of the previous evening. Given his hangover, he was in no condition for bushwhacking and would have been content to stay in the truck and do a visual check from there.

He was considering his options when he arrived at the pull off spot and was leaning toward ignoring it when he noticed that the path leading to the clearing showed signs of recent use. Brush, primarily the golden rod and sumac on either side of the path, was mashed down, a clear indication that something big had used the path sometime over the weekend. Getting out of the truck, Moses closely inspected the ground for deer tracks but could not see any. This was not surprising since, while as Moses, with his scraggy beard, oily baseball cap, flannel shirt and bib overalls looked like a central casting type of mountain man, he was anything but an expert outdoorsman. His appearance had more to do with lack of hygiene and apathy about wardrobe than any attempt to fill any role. Not that his tracking ability or lack thereof would have made any difference anyway since, had there been tracks, they would not have survived the previous night's rain. However, he did know that if deer had used the path and if one had been a buck, there was a good chance of spotting antler rubs on some of the scrub brush along the way. Therefore, hangover or no, a hike to the pond was unavoidable.

As he went further down the path, checking both sides for rubs, he could not help but notice there was an increasingly larger amount of disturbed brush as he went further from the road. Even with his nominal amount of experience, he could see that something big had taken place within the last day or two. Excited, he figured he had better check closer to the little pond, in case a couple of bucks had fought in the clearing. Someplace in his distant past, Moses had read in an outdoor magazine about these duels and how often the bucks could get their antlers locked together.

Now wouldn't that be somethin'? Moses thought, ignoring his pounding head and increasing his pace in anticipation.

As he neared the clearing beside the pond, Moses found the shortest route blocked by a mass of brambles. In a hurry and rather than go around he decided to push his way straight through, which is how he put is foot right in the middle of the dead man's chest.

****

There was a dead coyote lying on the west side of Route 618. Jimmy Kalid noticed it as he was driving north, made a U-turn, and came back to check it out. He had seen one or two of these animals from a distance but never up close, so he did not want to pass up this chance. Flipping on his hazard lights, he pulled his C-J5 onto the shoulder and got out.

It looked like a miniature version of a German shepherd. Either a female or young adult, it probably would have stood no more than fifteen to eighteen inches at the shoulder— large for a western coyote but, given that this was New York State, not especially big for the eastern subspecies. Its death had been, judging by the flattened head, mercifully quick, probably done in last night's rain or this morning's fog since the body was still in good shape.

I wonder if whoever hit it knew what he did. Jimmy thought, *Probably they thought it was someone's pet dog and never stopped to check it out.*

Jimmy reached down and stroked the dead animal, feeling the soft underfur. Rising, he considered throwing it in the back of his Jeep and taking it with him to school. Maybe it would stimulate his ninth grade English students to write something of interest. Then again, carrying a large dead animal past massed high school students and up to the second floor at eight o'clock on a Monday morning would probably mess up the day, if not the week. So he reconsidered. Instead, using his foot, he moved the body off the edge of shoulder into the grass. That is when he saw the note lying under the hindquarters.

Printed in block letters, the note read, "DISTROY THESE." Nothing more: bad spelling, no salutation, no signature.

However, there was something recognizable about the stationery. Someone had removed the letterhead and from the looks of the job, they had probably cut it off with a paper cutter. Whoever had done it apparently had been in a hurry and left just enough color and ink so if one was familiar with the stationery, they could tell that it came from Kaaterskill Central School's district office. Jimmy had seen enough memorandums and directives under that letterhead in his three years at the school to identify the source.

Jimmy laughed at the misspelling, crumpled up the note and, not wishing to litter, tossed in on the Jeep floor behind the front seat.

Back in the vehicle, he made another U-turn and headed in to school leaving the coyote carcass to the crows. It was the first Monday morning of October and he did not want to start off the month by being late. Besides, today, of all days, he wanted to make sure he had time to stop in the faculty room before going upstairs to his classroom.

****

Jimmy Kalid was the youngest member in terms of age and service, to be teaching in the KCS High School English department and, as such, his assignment was to teach whatever courses the more tenured teachers did not want. This meant four sections of Ninth Grade English. His fifth preparation was the one and only section of Advanced Placement English. While this latter assignment appeared to be a plum for such a young teacher, it was not really the case. The truth was that none of the other three high school English teachers had the time nor the inclination to do the work required to handle the six or seven seniors taking this course. They simply were not interested in teaching it so it fell to the rookie. To Jimmy it was a challenge and he enjoyed having to shift intellectual gears once a day—*speeding up my brain* was the way he thought of it.

In addition to teaching five courses, Jimmy, as well as the rest of the faculty, had other mandatory duties. First thing every morning some had to supervise and take attendance in a homeroom while those without a homeroom were required to do bus duty. This duty necessitated watching students disembark from the buses and making sure they were not bringing any contraband to school. Given that most all the students had large backpacks with which they could sneak just about anything short of a fully assembled AK-47 into the building, this vigilance was not a much of a deterrent. When they thought about it this was unsettling to those whose job was to intercept smuggled goods. During the school day, all teachers were required to monitor one study hall and check bathrooms for tobacco or pot use whenever they passed a "john" on their way up or down the hall. In addition, they had to supervise either the gymnasium or the outdoor campus, depending on the weather, during two of their lunch hours each week.

Jimmy was one of the fortunate few who had a homeroom. In his case a section of thirty ninth graders. However, because he did not coach an interscholastic sport team, Jimmy had to put in at least two evenings a month chaperoning the school's students at extracurricular events. To facilitate the assignment of this duty, the school's assistant principal posted a sign-up sheet in the faculty room at the beginning of each month with a listing of all the upcoming athletic and social events. The staff was required to choose the two events on a first come, first serve basis or face being assigned to those no one wanted. Since this was a new month it meant Jimmy's attendance was required at— he had a choice of two and in any combination—a football, soccer, field hockey game or a dance following one of the two home football games. But, because he had been busy getting ready for the new school year, he had neglected to place his name on this month's list during the previous week, thus the need to get to the faculty room.

He did not want a situation like occurred two years ago. As a new teacher in the district, he was ignorant of this requirement so failed to sign up for any duty in September and was forced into a last minute cancellation of a Friday date in order to fulfill his duties. His date, a psych major at SUNY Oneonta, had not been the least bit understanding and that was the last time he heard from her.

****

"Too late, my boy, the football games are all taken. Looks like its field hockey or soccer. Nothin' like a spirited field hockey or soccer game on a cold day, especially if it's rainin' or, better still, snowin'." The speaker was Mike Case who had settled into the most comfortable chair in the room, a cup of coffee on the table beside him. As usual Mike had a smile on his face and traces of his breakfast dribbled over the front of his sweatshirt.

Mike Case was "a local boy makes good" story. Having graduated from KCS 10 years ago, he went on to a small liberal arts college in the Midwest that had open admissions—meaning admission was open to anyone able to pay the tuition and students could remain enrolled until the money ran out or they graduated—whichever came first. After nine semesters, Mike found he had inadvertently passed enough courses that he was in imminent danger of graduating and, as such, needed to declare a major. When this requirement was made known to him, Mike thought *Oh my God, what am I going to do now?* After a quick check of the options, he chose physical education, probably because he found PE was easy to spell. When, two years later, he had finally accumulated enough credit hours, the college actually conferred a degree on him. This forced him to leave the campus. Having no place else to go, he returned home to Snyder's Corners.

At this point, his father, who owned the biggest bluestone quarry in the area, informed Mike that he had paid too much to let him idle around and he—Mike—had better either get a job or come to work in the bluestone mine. Mike, having seen enough men with missing fingers and toes and not wanting to join them, applied for the recently opened high school physical education job at KCS and was accepted. Given that he got along well with everyone and the fact that he was a KCS alumnus, he fit in well with the faculty, students, and, most importantly, the administration. The administration and board of education saw no problem in giving him tenure after his third year. The fact he had coached three consecutive winning basketball teams helped. This was especially important, since it made it easier to ignore the fact that the person in charge of the high school physical education was five-foot eight inches tall and weighed close to 300 pounds.

****

"I don't mind the field hockey games, but you're right, it's a lot better if the weather's good." Jimmy brushed past Mike's outstretched legs and, digging a pen out of his shirt pocket , signed his name on the schedule for the field hockey games next Thursday and the following Wednesday.

"Yeah, watchin' those young girls runnin' around in those kilts isn't bad," Mike's smile was now a cross between a grin and a leer. " 'specially if it's Katie Lasher. Otherwise, it's a lot like watchin' grass grow."

"Hadn't noticed." Jimmy lied.

Actually, as far as Katie Lasher was concerned, he had noticed. Katie was in his AP class, a senior, all everything whether it was sports or academics and the proof that genetics can be wrong—both her parents were KCS dropouts. In fact, while she lacked nothing in athletic and academic ability, she was also tops in good looks and personality. Easily the most popular girl in the school with both her peers and the faculty, she had only one flaw as far as the boys were concerned. She ignored all of them.

Jimmy's mind was drifting between Katie and AP English as he went across the room for his first cup of coffee of the day. Tossing a quarter into the collection pot and taking his cup off the wall rack, he waited while another teacher milled around in confusion in front of the coffee urn.

"May I help you?" Jimmy asked.

"Where are the coffee cups?" The teacher was dressed in a long green dress, her blond hair done up in a bun, and she wore no make up or jewelry. Jimmy did not recognize her as being anyone he had seen around school before.

"Unless you're a regular, you will probably have to go to the cafeteria and ask for a Styrofoam cup."

"Sorry, I'm afraid I don't know the rules. I'm substituting today for Mr. Meyers. This is the first time I've been in this building. How do I get to the cafeteria?" The poor woman looked like she was badly in needed of a cup of coffee so Jimmy felt sorry for her.

"It's just a couple of steps down the hall. Why don't you wait here? I'll go get one for you." With that, he went out the twenty or so steps to the cafeteria and begged the cooks, who were busy dicing carrots that were to be mixed with cans of assorted meats to form the basis for that day's stew, to get him a cup.

Returning he asked. "What's the problem with Milt?"

****

Milt Meyers was the eighth grade English teacher. Jimmy was not sure how long Milt had been teaching at KCS but he was on the staff and tenured when Jimmy started. Even though Meyers taught in the same area, although technically in the Junior High English Department, and was responsible for the lead-up courses to those Jimmy taught, the two rarely spoke. This was not a rare occurrence since Meyers tended to be a loner and ignored everyone. On those rare occasions when he showed up in the faculty room, he would take a seat in a corner and spend the time with his nose stuck in a novel. Unusual for an English teacher, no one ever remembered seeing him correcting papers.

This was not typical for most teachers who felt the faculty room was the best place to get caught up on class related work without being interrupted by students, or to blow off steam generated by either the students or the job in general. Jimmy learned early on that one of the best ways to get a "feel" for handling students, especially those he considered difficult, was to talk it out with a group of his peers. Usually there was at least one other teacher who had found a way to reach that child and they were willing to share their knowledge. In addition, someone's problem would often generate one or more solutions that would improve a newcomer's technique in both teaching and solving the problems put forth by the local or state mandates. Of course also, much of what sounded like trashing of the students and district was just the way for teachers to handle the stress generated by the job's many frustrations. This way one could relieve pressure with those who understood this stress and it was an unwritten rule of the faculty room that none of it left there. While to an outsider, it might seem as though there was a lot of bickering and complaining going on amongst the faculty members, there was also a lot of give and take that added to the ongoing training of each teacher, provided, of course, the individual was willing to participate. Milt seemed immune to this.

In addition, Milt's behavior carried over to other areas where he should have interacted with his fellow teachers. During joint Junior High/High School English Department meetings, he would sit in the back, read a book, and never contribute to discussions on either curriculum or students. Moreover most of the faculty tried on a regular basis to get together socially. This included a regular Friday afternoon celebration where they took over one end of the Snyder's Corners Tavern's barroom and calling it POETS Corner—an anagram for Piss On Everything Tomorrow is Saturday. Although he had been asked,

Meyers never joined them. Word was he had served in the Special Forces during Vietnam War and was still doing weekend warrior stuff. There was a rumor circulating in the school that he and the Chief School Officer had some kind of history and that helped Meyers keep his job. Whether this was true or not, Jimmy had little opinion one-way or the other about Meyers. Since he had not seen otherwise, Jimmy just assumed Meyer must be a good disciplinarian which, given he was teaching eighth grade, was a plus. How good a teacher he was, was open to discussion.

****

"I'm not sure. All I know is that I got a call last week that they needed a sub for Mr. Meyers." She filled the cup, dumped in some cream and several spoons of sugar. "My name is Phyllis Nielsen, by the way. And thank you for getting me the cup."

"Jimmy Kalid" He offered his hand. "I teach the next level up, ninth grade English. If you need any help, I'm in room two-seventeen. Those eighth grade kids can be tough on subs so give a holler."

"Oh, I'm sure I won't have any problem, but if I do, I'll give you a call." She pulled out a map of the school from the "substitute teacher packet", studied it for a moment and, with coffee in hand, went out the door.

Jimmy did not have the nerve to tell her about the administration's rule that prohibited teachers from taking coffee or food outside of the faculty room or cafeteria.

Chapter 2

The first period class was fifty-six minutes of Hell for twenty-four ninth grade students, fifteen of which were boys and only a few of whose parents had graduated from high school—the rest had dropped out, usually after eighth grade. This was one of three sections of English 9 designated as "regular". The fourth section was "advanced", meaning it consisted of students whose parents actually cared about their children's education—this section also had the smallest number of students. Students in the "regular" classes rarely matriculated beyond high school, assuming they graduated at all, which meant most of the students did not really want to be there.

These designations of "regular" and "advanced" were more for pubic consumption than any particular criteria. While, in general, students were assigned based on ability, usually to be classified had as much to do with your parents' interest in the school as it did with their child's performance. It was a standing joke amongst the faculty that if the school ever created a "slow" group it would require using the school's auditorium as a classroom to hold them.

While there were students in the "regular" sections that were capable of better work and going beyond high school, it required an astute teacher to single them out and encourage them. Unfortunately, most teachers missed these students because they were too tired and harassed from just trying to get their classes to sit still long enough to teach the students anything much less offer much encouragement to individual students. As a result, the students in these lower sections simply went

11

in lockstep until they either dropped out or graduated with a minimal local diploma. They then joined their parents on the welfare rolls.

Jimmy, being new to the education field and still naive, was hoping to use the dead coyote incident to try to reach and stimulate his first period class. Like all good teachers, Jimmy spent more time trying to motivate his students to learn than actually teaching them. Just trying to balance this while maintaining enough discipline so those motivated could be taught was a battle that left him exhausted by the end of most days.

"Have any of you every seen a coyote up close?" he asked.

"Nope, but sometimes we hear them howlin' up on ole Henry Hudson Mountain behind our house." said Kathy Brink.

"They's bayin' at the moon." Billy Schultz offered "We hear 'em all the time. 'Specially in the spring when they's runnin' down fawns. My daddy says that's why there ain't as many deer 'round as there useta be."

"Grandfather says that the coyote is a spirit helper. He's a trickster that makes things appear different than they really are. Grandfather says that the coyote will sometimes give a person clues to mysteries that have happened or will happen." This came from Josh Fisher, usually a quiet, introspective boy.

****

Josh's grandfather was a Native American and a bit of a mystic. Having grown up on the reservation, the old man had either left on his own volition or was expelled by the tribe over his difference of opinion about their building a casino. He built a cabin up on Hendrick Hudson Mountain where he spent most of the year hunting and fishing. Twice each year he would come down from the mountain to cash his tribal royalty checks and spend the day at the Snyder's Corners Tavern drinking and complaining about the way the whites treated his people and the way tribal members treated each other. Once the tirade was over and, after spending the night in the sheriff's lockup to sober up, he would disappear back onto his mountain for another six months.

****

"That's interesting, Josh, maybe you should write about that sometime." Jimmy's comments brought a smile to the young boy's face.

"That's just Injun stuff. Don't mean nothin.'" Billy Schultz did not sound impressed.

Ray Dienst's hand shot up. Jimmy pointed to him.

"Yeah Mr. K. My Dad shot one a couple of years ago. Right off of our back porch. Wanna know why?"

"Why was that, Ray?" Jimmy was hoping for something that could be used for a story.

"Caught it tryin' to hump our coon dog."

That lowered the bar.

"What did he wanta screw the dog for?" Like most ninth grade boys, Eddie Graef, who hid out in the back row, was waiting for some way to put a sexual spin on the conversation.

"My dad says that's how they get coy dogs." Ray again.

"According to what I've recently read, the coyotes we have around here aren't coy dogs but are more closely related to wolves." Jimmy was thinking that he had made a mistake and was trying to get the class back on topic.

"That's scary—like in the three little pigs or little Red Ridin' hood." Melvin Cranks was trying to get a laugh. Unfortunately, it went over the heads of the rest of the class, most of whom had not had parents who read them the classic children's book—or much else, for that matter.

"I hear they kill cats." Susan Mower blurted out, with out bothering to raise her hand; a sure sign that Jimmy was not gaining control.

"Timmy Griffin kills cats." That was Mary Graves.

"I don't neither. That's a lie!" Timmy's voice was high pitched but, somehow, menacing.

"Timmy Griffin would hump coyotes." Eddie Graef again, just loud enough for Timmy to hear but, hopefully not the teacher.

"That would get us coy Griffins." That came from Fred Brant and generated laughter from all the boys and a few of the girls.

Timmy Griffin did not have a long fuse. Actually, Timmy had no fuse at all. Not locally born and raised, his parents having moved up from Babylon, New York a year ago, he was considered an outsider by most of the ninth graders and a target for harassment. To make matters worse, had his parents stayed on Long Island or were KCS a suburban school, Timmy probably would have been diagnosed as having Attention Deficit Disorder and been dosed up to his eyeballs with Ritalin. Since this was not the case at KCS, Timmy was left alone to act on his feelings. This time it meant jumping out of his seat and charging Fred. Grabbing Fred around the neck, Timmy began banging the much larger boy's head against the window.

I wonder if the window is going to break before I can get there? Jimmy though as he made his way past the overturned desk to where the altercation was taking place. He grabbed Timmy by the arms and pulled him off Fred. This proved to be a big mistake.

With Timmy's arms pinned, he was unable to block the punch thrown by Fred. The fist caught Timmy square on the nose, which immediately began leaking blood.

"Damn that hurts!" Timmy reached up to hold his nose, noticed the blood and began to cry.

"You," Jimmy pointing at Timmy "get to the nurse's office! Fred, you stay right there. We'll talk after class!"

Then on second thought. "Ray, maybe you'd better go with Timmy to the nurse, just to make sure he gets there OK." Jimmy was not concerned about Timmy passing out physically on the way to the nurse's clinic but that he might take a detour by way of his home. It was necessary to watch these kids carefully or they would escape.

With Fred sitting sullen in the chair next to the window and the overturned desks and chairs righted, the rest of the class gradually calmed down. As altercations go, this was a comparatively short one and relatively easily controlled. After all, it was a Monday in October. If it had occurred on a Friday in June, the result might well have been bloodier. Perhaps it would have ended even deadly.

"Now get out your text books and go to page fifty-six. We're going to diagram sentences."

The class gave a collective sigh; the fun was over, which meant getting back to work.

When the bell rang, ending the class, Jimmy stopped Fred on his way out. "You'll be spending Tuesday's and Thursday's lunch hours here with me."

"What for, I didn't do nothin'? Why are ya pickin' on me? It was that Timmy that started it. How come nothin's happenin' to him?"

"First of all, you did start something by calling Timmy a name. Second, as soon as I catch up to Timmy, I'm going to assign him the same noon hour detention."

Of course, Jimmy could have let the assistant principal handle the discipline but he had learned a long ago that was not the best way for a teacher make a good impression on the administration. As a rule, most principals wanted nothing to do with discipline. In fact, they considered it an imposition on their day. Having a student arrive at the office in need of discipline, meant the principal had to interact with the student, teacher, and, in the worst cases, a parent. Moreover, it also meant making a decision, something most principals avoided at all cost. Therefore, if a teacher sent a child to the office for disciplinary reasons, the principal chose to interpret it to mean the teacher could not control his or her class and placed a memo to that effect in the teacher's folder. This would reappear in the teacher's year-end evaluation. If, by the time the teacher reached their third, tenure year, and he or she had too many of these memos, this often tipped the balance against granting tenure. Consequently, Jimmy handled his own discipline, generally by assigning noon hour detention on those days he did not have lunch duty—after school detention might have been better deterrent but, since most students rode the bus, this was prohibited. After three years of teaching, Jimmy had learned to eat his lunch quickly; to hell with digesting it.

****

Sheriff William "Moe" Mozeski was not a happy man. For the second time this year, the board of supervisors had just ordered him to cut his budget. This meant he would have to let another deputy go, reduce another to part time and cut one all-night patrol. When he was elected Sheriff of Palatine County three years ago, the Sheriff's force consisted of a dozen deputies, now he was down to half that number and one of those was about to be laid off. Given the Sheriff's Department was the only law enforcement agency in the county that meant the citizens were going to have to do with a lot less protection. Of course, there were always the State Police but their nearest substation was over in Oneonta and they did not have many men to spare either. The third alternative would have been a Snyder's Corners' police force. But this was no longer an option. The Snyder's Corners' village council had disbanded their two-man police force five years ago in response to a budget crunch and a report that the chief was a little too interested in preteen girls. So the county sheriff was the thin blue line that stood between honest citizens and criminals in the whole area.

Let some county supervisor's house get burglarized, Moe thought, *and he'll want me and/or a couple of deputies at his place ASAP.*

It was not that Palatine County was a hotbed of crime. Most of the Sheriff's calls came as a result of motor vehicle/deer collisions. For the last three years, Palatine County had led the state in incidents of deer-caused accidents. This was an interesting statistic considering the relative sparseness of the county's population. In fact, one wag even suggested that Palatine County use the deer-crossing silhouette as a logo on the county's official stationery.

The second most common source of calls dealt with DWI accidents. Apparently, when the citizens of the county were not running into deer, they were boozing it up and running into each other. Moe always figured that if he wanted to raise some quick cash, all he had to do was park his car in the middle of Route 618 and eventually, someone would run into it. Considering the odds that the driver would be drunk meant a big insurance payoff; it could be better deal than playing the lottery. Of course too, considering the lack of employment, there was also a good chance that the driver would be without insurance which would have negated the whole thing.

Moe was in the midst of this line of thinking when the 911 call came in—there was a body out by Loomis Pond. Realizing that the nearest deputy was way the hell over on the other side of the county, Moe decided he might as well take the call. This was actually a good break since it would allow him more time to consider his choices and he could use some time out of the office.

Loomis Pond was about two miles from his office and, just for the hell of it, Moe considered using the siren and the roof lights. It was rare that he had an opportunity to go full out. The only problem was that since the distance was so short it would be a problem getting up to speed and then slowing down in time, so he reconsidered and drove at a lower speed. It did not make any difference anyway since the Snyder's Corners ambulance and EMT's had beaten him to the scene.

After parking the cruiser safely off the pavement, Moe hiked in to the pond. On the way through the trampled brush, he was wondering what to expect. Since this was the fall of the year, chances were that some downstate hunter who, while scouting deer cover, had keeled over with a heart attack. It happened every year, usually the first day of deer season, when some guy with high blood pressure, cholesterol numbers off the charts and whose idea of exercise was to forego the remote and walk across the room to shut off the TV, would traipse off into the woods to have a massive coronary. Usually though when this kind of thing happened it was much further into the woods and on a lot lousier day.

Moe arrived just in time to see one of the EMT's zip the body bag closed. "What we got?" he asked.

"Not anyone I know—guess you'd call it a John Doe." Moe recognized the EMT as John Cobb's youngest son.

"Lemme see." Moe said leaning over the stretcher and unzipping the bag far enough to expose the face.

The John Doe was a young male, probably in his late 20's or early 30's, dark hair, kind of southern European looking. From what Moe could see the guy was dressed in a suit and a tie.

Although, given how he was dressed it hardly seemed possible, Moe still had to ask. "Heart?"

"I doubt it." said Cobb, "Not unless he had the attack and then crawled into that mess of blackberry bushes to die. Christ, I'll be pickin' thorns and stickers outa me for the next week. 'Sides, he has a lot of blood on the back of the head. My guess would be someone hit him with somethin'. Did you see too that he was wearin' a suit? What'n hell would a guy be out here in a suit for?"

"Yeah, I noticed the suit. Your guess is as good as mine. Maybe he had a call of nature. Was his fly open?" This last caused both EMT's to chuckle. "Well, might as well get him to Doc Condro. Let's see what he comes up with."

Dr. Edward Condro was the local, general practitioner and, because there was no medical examiner's office in Palatine County, he was what passed for as the county's revolving coroner. Out of necessity brought on by budget constraints, the county did not have a full-time coroner or even one that was on call, so whatever doctor was closest to an accidental death scene was automatically "volunteered" for the job. When no one was available, it meant taking the body over to

Fox Hospital in Oneonta for the autopsy and the county board of supervisors did not like that. It cost the county more money.

"We're on our way." Cobb, still laughing to himself, grabbed one end of the stretcher while his partner grabbed the other. Since the ground was too wet and tangled to make the stretcher's wheels of any use, they were straining under the weight of body and stretcher. With a collective groan, they lifted and began the hike back to the parked ambulance.

"By the way, who found him?" Moe called after the EMT's.

"Moses Barkman" said the trailing EMT, "he's back by the road sittin' in his truck."

"Thanks, tell him to stick around, I'll be right out to talk to him in a minute.

Moe made a cursory check of the area. There was not too much to see. He figured the rescue crew had trampled down the grass around the bramble patch but there had been no reason for them to protect the scene, especially with no law enforcement person there to tell them to take it easy. It might have been nice, though, to know whether the body had been dumped before or after last night's rain. Whether the ground under it had been wet or dry would have been a clue but now, of course, it was too late. Likewise, if there had been any tracks, the rain of the previous night would have washed them away so the EMT's tracks would be all there was to see anyway.

From what he could see though, Moe guessed the John Doe died some place else and then had been dumped there—the brambles were too thick for someone to have gotten in there voluntarily. In fact, it would have probably taken no more than two people to toss the body into the bushes—one if he were strong enough and did not mind a couple of scratches. Moe started back toward the road when he noticed a buck rub on a sumac right next to the trail. Being, like most males in the county, a hunter, he stopped for a closer look. On this closer inspect, he realized that he had been wrong; it was not a buck rub unless the buck had green paint covered antlers. Taking his trusty Swiss Army knife out of his pocket he carefully cut the branch

19

off, paint and all, and put it in a plastic bag he kept in his pocket just in case he ever needed it. This had been the first time.

Back at the road, he found a sober Moses Barkman sitting in his truck. Moses filled Moe in about how he found the body; not that it added much of anything that would help. Moe thanked him and, making a U-turn, went back to the office. He had to get hold of the State Police Bureau of Criminal Investigation to have their lab check the origin of the paint.

Chapter 3

Jimmy was coming out of school at the same time Phyllis was leaving.

"How did your day go?" he asked, "Kids didn't give you any trouble did they?"

"Trouble? No. But there wasn't much of any teaching to do. All I did was show the same movie, *Pride and Prejudice*, over and over again, all day. Maybe the kids weren't bored, but I sure was." Phyllis gave a long sigh which was followed by a smile.

Meyers had the reputation of showing a lot of movies to his classes. While they included classics like *Romeo and Juliet, Gone With the Wind*, and *To Kill a Mockingbird*, there were others that didn't have any redeeming social value or immediate importance to the English 8 curriculum. Among Meyers' favorites were *The Green Berets, Walking Tall, To Hell and Back*, and everything Vin Diesel ever made. As far as Jimmy could ascertain Meyers never did any follow-up on the films, neither giving reading/writing assignments based on them nor even discussing them in class. By way of example, when Jimmy asked in his ninth grade "regular" class who wrote *Romeo and Juliet*, no one had any idea. Apparently, Milt just subjected his students to as much of the movie as the class period allowed, released them and then shown the remainder the next time the classes met. An especially long epic, like *Lawrence of Arabia* or *Ben Hur* could take a full week. It was a joke among the rest of the faculty that you could tell when kids left Meyers' class because they were blinking in the light like startled owls or bears just coming out of hibernation.

"Yeah, Milt likes his VCR, alright. Are you coming back tomorrow?"

"I expect to be here for two weeks. At least that's what they told me in the office. Apparently Mr. Meyers has some sort of military exercise and will be out until a week from next Monday."

"Ok, I'll see you again tomorrow morning then. By the way, if you think of it and since you're going to be here that long, maybe you should bring in your own coffee cup." Jimmy climbed into his Jeep, smiled and waved as he drove out of the parking lot.

"Thanks, I'll try to remember." Phyllis smiled and waved back. As she watched Jimmy drive away she thought, *Hmm, nice buns. Maybe this week won't be too bad after all.*

****

Phyllis Nielsen was on the run from the worst possible combination: a broken heart and a boring job. At the age of twenty-two, she had graduated *summa cum laude* from The University of Minnesota with a Master's degree in early childhood psychology and had immediately taken a job as an elementary school guidance counselor in a prestigious school in suburban Minneapolis. While she found the job boring—it mainly dealt with testing and evaluation of tests—she did make the acquaintance of and had an affair with, the elementary school principal. Eight torrid months later, the principal, after a romantic dinner and evening of sex, instead of asking Phyllis to marry him as she hoped, confessed that he was already married with no chance of divorce. Devastated, Phyllis kicked her lover out of her apartment, quit her job, sold all her worldly possessions, cleaned out her savings account and, with her cat, headed east. Two mornings later, while having coffee at a rest stop on the New York State Thruway, she picked up a discarded copy of the *Sunday New York Times* and saw an ad in the real estate section for a used, forty-foot mobile home on half an acre of land in upstate New York. She called the realtor listed in the ad and found the price to be doable. She immediately purchased the place, sight unseen. Unfortunately, she forgot to ask about the taxes, which were so high that the former owner was willing to sell at a reduced price just to get out from under them. At any rate, that is how Phyllis Nielsen ended up in a rusting Holiday Cottage in a clearing in the woods on the outskirts of Snyder's Corners with only what was left of her savings and no immediate plans to replenish them.

On impulse and since it was too late to apply for a regular job, she put her name in to substitute teach at Kaaterskill Central School in the hope that just maybe it would lead to some full-time work. When Phyllis' application landed on the desk of the secretary whose job it was to schedule substitutes, the secretary did mental handsprings. It was unusual for a qualified teacher of any kind, much less one with a master's degree, to put their name on the substitute list. Those who did were usually recent retirees who were looking to pick up the fifty-five-dollar per diem the job paid. The trouble with retirees was that they were not that reliable; when really needed during the winter months, they disappeared to warmer climes. That meant the district was constantly scrounging for subs and usually took anyone with a smattering of education past high school. In fact, on one occasion and back before it was necessary to fingerprint all school personnel to make sure they were not sex offenders, the school had actually hired, unbeknownst to them, a senior from Oneonta High School to substitute in physical education. The kid was doing really well, too, until a couple of his buddies showed up at KCS during the lunch hour and ratted him out. So as soon as the secretary checked with the school system in Minnesota to be sure Phyllis' credentials were legitimate and make sure Phyllis's personnel folder was moved into the New York State registry, she moved Phyllis' name to the top of the "to call" list. Meyers' fall military exercise was the first opening of the year.

****

Moe had again been busy trying to juggle deputy assignments when the phone on his desk rang. He managed to get it on the second ring.

"Sheriff Mozeski's office, the sheriff speaking."

"Moe, Doc Condro, I'm at the funeral home and have finished up your John Doe's autopsy. I think you better get over here."

Moe put down the phone and, it being a nice day and only a couple of hundred yards to the funeral home, decided he needed the exercise.

The John Doe's body laid facedown on the embalming table. A bit of matted blood was visible on the back of his head.

"Looks like he was conked over the head." Moe leaned over to get a closer look at the back of the man's head.

"Yeah, he was", replied Dr Condro, "but that's not what killed him."

"No?"

"No. It might have knocked him a bit silly, maybe even disoriented him, but it didn't kill him. Hell there's always a lot of blood on superficial head wounds." The doctor rolled the body over onto its back. "Check this out."

Moe notice a small round hole in the man's chest, just to the right of the left nipple. There was no blood.

"Bullet?"

"Guess again." Then the doctor chuckled. "Oh hell, you'd never guess anyway. It's a hole made by a pencil."

"A what?"

"A pencil, specifically a number-two pencil. What I figure was he either fell on, or was stabbed with, a pencil. It went through his chest and punctured the aorta. Most of the blood ran into his chest cavity. He either died from loss of blood or suffocated from the pressure on his lungs. Was a mess of it in his chest when I went in to get this."

Dr Condro held up a plastic bag; inside was a yellow, number-two, Ticonderoga pencil, sharpened to a point.

Moe turned the bag over, concentrating on the object inside. "Are you sure? It doesn't seem possible."

"Moe", the doctor was grinning, "I'm eighty-five years old and have been a GP for the last sixty of those years, and every time I think I've seen it all, something like this comes up to prove me wrong."

"And you think that was possible?" Moe was slowly turning the plastic bag with the pencil.

"Anything is possible." Doc was smiling. "You heard about that Australian crocodile hunter guy a month or so ago?"

"Steve Irwin? Yeah, got killed by a sting ray barb through the heart." Moe looked from the body to Doc "Are you sayin' that same thing happened here?"

"I'd be guessin' but it could be the same kinda thing."

"But how?", Moe was puzzled.

"Well, I'm guessin' again, but judgin' from this hole in the pocket of his suit I'd say the pencil was in this pocket." Dr. Condro held up John Doe's suit jacket, turned it inside out and poked his finger from inside the inner pocket out through a hole in the lining. "Somehow, maybe as the result of that blow on the head, he was knocked forward and the pencil went from his pocket into his chest. Apparently it was lined up just right so it missed any ribs and went straight to the aorta."

"Geez, what are the chances of that—one in a million?"

"Probably—the guy shoulda played the lottery."

"So, what's your best guess? Homicide?"

"You're the detective so you'll have to figure that out, but I suspect the actual death was an accident. In fact, I'd bet whoever hit him didn't even know the cause of death. My best guess is that you're probably looking at manslaughter."

"So you figure he was hit first, then fell on the pencil?"

"From the forensic evidence, I'd say so. Once that pencil hit the aorta, he bled out pretty fast, too fast to have pumped that much blood to that head wound."

"Well there is one thing; he sure as hell didn't dump himself in the bushes out by Loomis Pond. Somebody's got to know how, when and where this happened."

"You're right on that, Moe, besides, the location of that head injury is a pretty good indication he didn't do it to himself. I doubt too that he could have somehow struck his head on somethin' and then fallen forward onto the pencil. Think you'll get any prints off that?" Doc asked pointing to the plastic bag in Moe's hand.

"I doubt it, too thin for one thing and when it went through his chest, it probably wiped off anything usable."

Moe gave another, cursory look at the body. As he did, he noticed there was black ink on the victim's right hand.

"I see Sid's finished up here."

"Yeah, Boyce stopped in about 20 minutes ago and took finger prints. He figured he would get them checked sometime this afternoon. He said he'd been by to see you too."

"Yeah, I called them earlier and he stopped in just before he came here. I had a paint sample I wanted the BCI lab to check out. May mean somethin', then again maybe it doesn't. Well, better get back to the office in case there's some word about who our boy is. You might as well leave the body here; as soon as we know who we're dealin' with I expect there'll be someone around to claim it. By the way, you didn't find any kind of ID in his clothes, by chance?"

"I went through everythin' fairly thoroughly." Doc indicated the wet pile of clothes. "Unless his name is Sears or JC Penny there isn't any identification on him. If he had a wallet, whoever dumped him took it."

"OK, thanks." Moe put the plastic bag in his shirt pocket and shook his head. "I'll be damned... a pencil." he still did not quite believe it.

"Yup', said Doc, "just like the kind kids use to take tests."

"I don't imagine you have any idea how long he's been dead?"

"Hell, Moe, I'm just a small town, country doctor, not Gil Grissom and this" he gestured to the embalming table, "isn't exactly a CSI crime lab. It's been cool and rainin' for the last couple of days so the body hasn't deteriorated that much, but still, I'd just be guessin'. That said, my best guess would be that, at the most, he's been dead no more than four days; at the least, two. I do know," the doctor pointed to the pile of clothes on the floor, "that he was there over night. His suit was soaked."

Moe chuckled. "Nothin' like statin' the obvious. So you're sayin' he died sometime between Thursday and Saturday?"

"That would be my guess. Of course, if you want a better answer you could send the body in to Albany. They've got a good forensics lab there and they could probably give you a better estimate. Wouldn't hurt my feelin's any."

"Yeah, but if it costs the county any extra money, the supervisors would be all over my ass about it. I'll take your word for it. Besides, that two day window is close enough."

Moe started out the door, stopped, and turned back to the doctor.

"One other thing, you said there was a lot of blood in his chest, does that mean there wouldn't be much at the scene?"

"Probably not, the pencil kinda formed a plug and kept all the blood in the guy's chest. I expect that, unless some of the blood from the head wound found its way to the ground, there probably wasn't much of a mess wherever it happened."

"Shit, that's gonna make it a lot tougher." Moe shook his head and went out the door.

****

It was the next morning when Investigator Sidney Boyce knocked on Moe's office door. The door was partially open so as soon as he knocked it swung back far enough so Moe could see who was there.

"Come on in, Sid." Moe was sitting at his desk still working on the same schedule.

Senior Investigator Sidney Boyce, New York State Police, Bureau of Criminal Investigation, entered the room and stood in front of Moe's desk.

Damn, Moe thought, *how do they do it? My deputies change into their uniforms in the locker room and by the time they get to their cars they look like they slept in them. On the other hand, these damn troopers would put in a full shift in a non-air-conditioned cruiser, on the hottest day in July and still have every crease in place. Must be something they're taught in Albany at the state police academy.*

"Mornin', Moe. How are the goats?" The State trooper inquired.

"They aren't goats, damn it, they're sheep." Sid Boyce was always busting Moe's chops about his wife's farm.

****

Moe Mozeski was not a Palatine County native. He had been a detective in the Dade County, Florida, Sheriff's Department when he met his wife, Grace (nee Snyder) Newkirk, while she and several of her girl friends were vacationing in Miami Beach to celebrate Grace's divorce becoming final. After a whirlwind courtship that lasted a week, the newly divorced farm girl from upstate New York married the native Floridian cop. It was a happy union. While Moe was not crazy about his job, he was good at it and they both liked Florida. They would have remained there indefinitely had it not been that Grace's father was gored to death by his prize bull. Grace, as an only child, inherited her father's dairy farm, lock, stock and outstanding bills. Since she could not handle the job of settling the estate alone, Moe quit his job and the two moved to Snyder's Corners.

Grace's family had a long history in Palatine County. Her great, great, great grandfather had first settled in the area in the early eighteen hundreds. Having actually been on his way to Wisconsin at the time, his covered wagon broke down for the third time since leaving the Hudson Valley while crossing the Delaware River. Tired of his wife's nagging him about his lack of ability as a mechanic, he dropped roots right there. This accident of history resulted in a town bearing his surname.

Back on the farm, it took Moe and Grace about one week to realize that, judging from the amount of debt her father had accumulated, operating a dairy farm in this area was a losing proposition and not anything either wanted to do. That decided, they sold off the herd—including the bull, which fetched top dollar—and machinery. They would have gotten rid of the land as well except Martha, Grace's daughter from her first marriage, suggested they might like to raise milking sheep. After Martha explained all the products that could be derived from the milk and wool as well as offering herself and her current boy friend as assistants, Grace jumped at the idea. Using the money from the sale of the stock and machinery, Grace purchased some breeding stock of East Friesen sheep and within two years, the Snyder Milking Sheep Farm was a huge success. Grace and her daughter were making excellent money selling cheese, milk-based soaps, yarn and knitted products both locally to tourists and over the Internet. On the other hand, Moe was not that happy with his part of the operation which consisted of helping with the lambing, putting up hay, and hauling packages to Oneonta to the UPS Store for shipping. He wanted something more fulfilling.

The opportunity came about rather suddenly. The Republican Sheriff was caught skimming money from fines leveled as the result of arrests made by his deputies. While this would not have bothered the local citizenry that much, the Sheriff, in an effort to increase his take, had insisted his deputies enforce the law that required a driver to have his headlights burning when windshield wipers were operating. This was a very easy violation to enforce since all that the deputies needed to do was to set up a roadblock on a rainy day along Route 618 and wave over those cars without their headlights on. Given that this was a law rarely enforced, the State Motor Vehicle Department was not especially looking for fines from the infraction so it made it easy for the Sheriff to keep this source of revenue for himself. With an average of one hundred stops per day at fifty dollars a pop, he had a nice rainy day fund working for him. Unfortunately, he failed to take into account that his actions was ticking off the electorate.

The citizens of Palatine County were especially incensed by the enforcement of this law since they felt this was an example the government interference. They figured that as long as they could see where they were going the government was not, by damn, going to tell them to turn on their headlights and wear down the bulbs and battery. When it happened that one of the deputies, tired of working in the rain without a cut, tipped off the State Attorney General's office, the Sheriff's scheme unraveled both legally and politically.

This combination of the State indicting the Sheriff for graft and the popular uprising against his enforcement of the wiper law gave the local Democratic Party hope of capturing the sheriff's position. With that in mind, they looked around for someone reasonably qualified to run against the incumbent. That search lead to Moe Mozeski. The race was tight but, primarily due to the wiper backlash, Moe managed just enough votes to win. The defeated sheriff ended up doing ten to twelve years in state prison for embezzlement.

While it got him away from the daily operation of the farm and back into some semblance of police work, there were headaches he had not anticipated. These mostly arose from the fact that, given this was upstate NY where the county board of supervisors was one hundred percent Republican, there was no chance that the supervisors were about to cut any out-of-state, Democratic sheriff any slack, even if his wife was from a founding father's family. Therefore, Moe and the supervisors were constantly at odds, the most recent budget cuts to his department being but one example.

The fact that he had a possible murder investigation on his agenda was almost a relief.

****

"Sit down and take a load off." Moe gestured to the chair in front of his desk. "What ya got for me?"

"A name, for one thing." The trooper slid a folder across the desk, sat down on the chair and put his hat in his lap.

Moe opened up the folder to read the report. The first thing to jump out at him was the name. "Joseph A. Scalani—damn a wop. Don't tell me the mob is startin' to use this area to dump bodies."

"I doubt it. We crosschecked with known mob members, especially anyone that we haven't seen for a while, right down to the guys on the street—nothing. In fact, you're not going to guess where we pulled the ID from."

"OK, so don't keep me guessin'. Where?"

"The New York State Teachers' Registry."

"Then the guy was a teacher?"

"'Was' is the working word here. He worked as an elementary teacher out in Hempstead Long Island for a year then quit two years ago"

"And?"

"Well, that's the damnedest thing; he quit that job and was working for the State Education Department out of Albany, in their Testing and Evaluation Division."

"Any idea why he turned up here?"

"We checked with his division and from what we found out yesterday afternoon, the guy took a couple of days off from work last week. Said he had to do some "personal business" and disappeared. Nobody in his office had heard from him since last Wednesday afternoon."

"Ok, now let's see what we got here: a guy from the State Education Department, Testing and Evaluation, no less, turns up dead in a field outside of Snyder's Corners and the cause of death is a number-two pencil in the chest." Moe laid the plastic bag with the pencil in it on top of the report. "I guess the next question is, are you going to handle this or am I?"

Boyce chuckled. "As interesting as it sounds, I guess it's going to be up to you even though, since he works for the State, he is one of our guys and we probably should be leading the investigation. The problem is we're short handed, especially in the BCI, since they have shipped a lot of our people downstate to keep an eye out for terrorists."

"You're short handed? Hell, the supervisors have cut me again so I'm down to five deputies and one of those is part time. How about we work together on this and share any information we can come up with?

"Ok, sounds good to me. Oh, by the way, about that paint." Boyce slid a second report across the table.

"Yeah?"

"Since you found it out in the middle of nowhere, I assumed it didn't come from a motor vehicle so I had the lab check it against All Terrain Vehicles. The DEC has a fairly good collection of samples they can use in cases of off-road damage. It proved to be a good assumption. They gotta match to a Polaris ATV, probably a 2003, 2004 or 2005." The Senior Investigator pointed to the lab results typed on the report. He was smiling, proud of himself for having guessed right.

"Oh great! Sid, do you know how many Polaris ATV's there are in this county? Hell, Big Ed Graef sells 'em by the hundreds out of his shop right here in town."

"I know there are at least two hundred of them registered in Palatine County alone because I checked already this morning."

"Damn Sid, that's just the registered ones—most guys never take 'em off their property so they don't bother with a license. That'll add another two hundred at least. Gonna be tough to narrow this search down."

"Well Moe, narrowing the search down is going to have to be your job since you're closer to Big Ed's than I am. When are you going to start?"

"Damned if I know, let me get back to you later."

Boyce got up, put on his hat and left. Moe tossed the schedule he had been working on to the other side of his desk and sighed.

Damn it, he thought, *this job never gets any easier.*

Chapter 4

Senior Investigator Boyce and the BCI were not 100 percent correct about the late Joseph (Joey) Anthony Scalani. Although Joey was not, nor never had been, a member of organized crime he was, in a way, connected to it. His uncle, the brother of Joey's mother, Isabel, was none other than Anthony (Two Toes) Torrelli. Although neither of Joey's parents ever informed Joey what his uncle did for a living, they had given Joey his uncle's name as a middle name. This was because Anthony and his wife, Clarissa, were unable to have children themselves and Joey's father felt it was a good idea to stay on the right side of his brother-in-law. The name and because Tony and Clarissa were Joey's godparents, had the effect of making Joey his uncle's favorite nephew. Consequently, Joey had a guardian angel in high (or low) places.

This was because Tony was a made member of the mob and bagman for none other than John Grotto. Since it was Tony's job to make sure Grotto's money got to the right people in the right places, he hated the title designation of "bagman". He much preferred "lobbyist", since his job in the state capitol, Albany, was to influence legislation. This was especially important when there was legislation pending that would affect those areas in which the mob had their special interests like construction, import/export, the Port of New York, and garbage. Tony was not only an important moneyman but, at five-foot, six inches and two hundred seventy pounds, he was a familiar figure around the state capitol building. Everyone from the governor down to the lowliest clerk knew Mr. Torrelli and gave him, if not respect, at least room.

Few, however, knew him well enough to call him "Two Toes", a nickname he got, not because of the last name of Torrelli but rather because he earned it when attempting his first and, as it turned out, last hit. Proving that just because someone owned a gun did not mean they could actually use it, he shot off three of the toes on his left foot when his .38 misfired. The intended target of the fusillade easily escaped. This made it obvious that Tony would not do well on this branch of the mob's career path so his immediate superior assigned him to their political department. Since Tony seemed to get along well with people and had a menacing air about him, he moved quickly up in the ranks, progressing from bribing New York City council members to Albany legislators. Had his mentor not been caught snitching to the Feds, a career move that got him whacked, Tony would probably have gone on to Washington. As a result of the loss of a patron, Tony's career stalled in Albany.

However, the problem with being an underling for a mob boss was that employment could be chancy, especially when your boss was under indictment for racketeering. When Grotto was convicted and sentenced to prison, Tony found himself unemployed. Taking his nest egg of money that he had skimmed, Tony "retired" from the mob and opened a small check cashing and loan sharking business in Jamaica, New York. It was a lucrative business and one that did not require too much of Tony's attention. Besides when his old buddies from the mob asked him where he was living, by telling them "Jamaica" it gave the impression he had retired to the Caribbean island. The fact that a balding, overweight, Italian who was supposedly living on a tropical island, was as pale as a sheet did not seem clue in his old compatriots.

Blissfully unaware of his godfather/uncle's mob connections, Joey grew up in Queens New York, as the son of a pizza parlor owner. All he remembered were the Christmas and birthday gifts showered on him by his Uncle Tony and Aunt Clarissa. If he ever wondered about his uncle's limp, he never asked.

A mediocre student at best, Joey barely graduated from high school but, since it was expected of all first generation Americans, he went on to college. He was accepted at C. W. Post on Long Island, not so much because of good high school grades but because, as a local resident, it would not put a particular strain on their limited dormitory facilities. In addition, since his uncle was more than happy to pay his tuition, money was no problem.

When it came to choosing a major, after a brief amount of thought, Joey opted for elementary education. He did this primarily because he liked the idea that teachers got two months of summer vacation that seemed, to him at least, to be a major benefit of the profession. Also, he figured the younger kids would be easier to work with since they knew less and, therefore, so did their teachers. Although it required some work to maintain a C average, Joey managed to graduate from Post in four years supplemented by a couple of summer school sessions. Upon receiving is diploma, he applied to teach fifth grade in one of the elementary schools in Hempstead. It was during his third year in this position that Joey found himself caught on the horns of an educational dilemma.

****

This dilemma was caused by an asinine State Education Department regulation that dictates that in order for a teacher in New York State to be permanently licensed they have to complete a master's degree program before they enter their fourth year of teaching. While the intent of the regulation is to give the appearance of well educated teaching staffs, what makes it asinine is that it not only causes an unfair burden on new teachers but is required at the wrong time in a teacher's career. What it does is to immediately send those who just graduated from college and, assuming they paid attention, know the latest educational research and content of their fields back for more of the same. On the other hand, those teachers in the field who have already permanently licensed are never required to go back for further education since there is no incentive, licensing or monetarily, for them to return to upgrade their skills.

Furthermore, there is no evidence that the more degrees in education a teacher has accumulated will make him or her a better educator. In fact, the opposite may be true since many of those with higher degrees tended to suffer more from analysis paralysis when, and if, they finally make an appearance in the classroom. The irony of the whole regulation lies in the fact that many of those who were responsible for it were taught by teachers who graduated from two-year, Normal Schools back in the first half of the twentieth century. These teachers, primarily female elementary teachers, had excellent success in teaching their youngsters with only a two-year associate's degree in education.

But the regulation is there so, reasonable or not, it must be complied with. Since teachers are neither born nor made but evolve from their work in the classroom, at a time when this latter experience should be the main focus of their growth, they have to concern themselves with more schooling. For teachers like Joey, the first four or five years should have been devoted to finding their way around the classroom, interacting with students, developing a method for getting the curriculum over to students and, quite simply, deciding if they made the correct career choice. Given the relative low pay and need to repay student loans, they do not need an extra financial burden at this point in their careers.

It would have been more sensible option to wait until a teacher completed five or more years in the field and then to require periodic updating of teaching techniques and their course knowledge. This could have been done by offering monetary incentives and time to encourage teachers with more years in education to take in-service or summer courses to update their skills. While, to some extent, some local districts do this, but since the Education Department leaves this to the discretion of local boards of education and given budget constraints, most opted to ignore this problem. Some districts simply will ask their teaching staffs to upgrade skills so they can be "be more professional"—an education euphemism for getting more work out of the teachers without paying for it.

So to comply with the State Department's master's degree requirement, a prospective teacher had two choices: either to stay in school to get the degree or, take immediate employment and get the degree within the next three years by taking graduate courses. In the former case, it means getting into a graduate program with the added expense of another year in college then entering a low paying field where it will be a large number of years before recouping that expense. In the latter case, it means holding down a full-time job in a new career while taking approximately half a semester's worth of graduate hours each year in the evenings, on Saturdays or during summer sessions. Therefore, between marking papers, doing lesson plans, and coping with the new experience of teaching students, these new teachers have to struggle with a minimum of ten graduate hours per year plus whatever travel time was required. In order to keep their sanity, most new teachers elect to give up their "summer vacation" to go back to graduate school. This means that had they been looking to supplement their incomes by taking summer employment they are not only without this income but have the added expenses of this schooling. In all, it was a lousy, bureaucratic decision made by out-of-touch people and proved a big stumbling block to some of those who would otherwise have made good, dedicated teachers.

****

Joey did not fall into this category since he was not nor ever would be an especially dedicated teacher. Rather it was giving up that precious summer vacation, not the money—he spent most of the summer months hanging with out-of-work friends anyway—that forced him out of teaching. Since his primary reason for getting into teaching was the summer-off perk, he was not about to give it up to go back to college. Therefore when, in his third year, a memo came down from the district office asking him whether he had completed his master's degree program and/or what his plans were for the meeting of this requirement before the upcoming September, he resigned his position. This left him at loose ends.

It was during the family's annual Fourth of July celebration that Joey explained his unemployment status to his uncle Tony. (The Scalani's and Torrelli's, as naturalized citizens who had made good, were big on celebrating the birth of the nation even though much of the money they made was sent to relatives back in Sicily for investment.)

Learning about his godson's lack of employment, Tony thought for a minute and then asked. "How about a job in the State Education Department?"

****

In 1967, Laurence J Peter published a book entitled *The Peter Principle* in which he proposed a theory of the same name. In its simplest interpretation, the "Peter Principle" says that within an organization people will advance one level beyond where they are competent. Some professional educators, however, have pretty much reversed this principle to one where as soon as this person reaches this level of incompetence and, unless pruned from the profession, he or she will advance up to the next higher level. Those in the field know this as "Those who can, teach; those who cannot teach, become administrators; and those who cannot administrate move into the State Education Department or, on occasion, go into colleges to teach education courses." Joseph Scalani was a good example of an educational professional who was about to enter this advanced form of the "Peter Principle."

****

While Joey had not been the best elementary teacher, he had not done any harm at that level, either. As a fifth grade teacher he had no state tests to evaluate his teaching and his students appeared to like him, especially because he gave them a lot of recess and require no homework—that would have meant he would have had to correct it. The fact that he gave high grades, especially to those students whose parents came to PTA meetings and/or had the ear of the board of education members, also worked to keep him well under the administration's radar. As such, he had no bad marks against his record, which meant he would get an excellent recommendation to the next level. The only real deterrent to his getting into the State Department was that, since he had no degree in educational administration he lacked the basic requirement to advance to this step. Fortunately, his uncle was able to cut some red tape for him.

Using his connections, Uncle Tony called a guy who knew a guy and within a couple of weeks of his applying, Joey's lack of qualifications was overlooked and he was hired. At this point Joey's resume landed on the desk of a clerk at the Education Department who was not a complete dolt. Having graduated from an area high school with BOCES degree in secretarial practice she was able to recognize Joey's talent. She found the perfect spot for him in the Department's Testing and Evaluation Division. Given that someone was needed to sort the incoming competency test answer sheets by school district and numerical scores, Joey seemed ideally qualified for the job. The fact that the job only needed his attention two times a year—February and September—when the test results were submitted, meant that Joey went from having two months of vacation to ten. He could not have been happier.

None of this information was available in the data banks of either the BCI or the State Education Department so was never going to be a part of either Sid's or Moe's investigation. Had they known, however, some of it might have been important.

****

The finding of the body out by Loomis Pond was common knowledge by Tuesday morning. In fact, it was topic One and One-A in every homeroom of the school. Jimmy Kalid's ninth graders were no exception.

"I heard ole Moses Barkman stepped right smack dab on it." Eddie Graef offered.

"Ugh!" This was in unison from a chorus of female voices.

"Imagine findin' a dead body that way?" Billy Schultz excitedly added.

"My dad said the guy was Eyetalian and he'd been hit in the head." This came from Billy Pierce who was the ninth grade authority on crime in Palatine County. His father, William (Bill) Pierce, was a deputy sheriff who was about to become the part time Palatine County deputy sheriff.

"I betcha he was knocked off by the mob 'n dumped here." Said Fred Brant. "I've seen that a lot on the Sopranos. The mob takes a guy on a ride 'n then bumps him off from the back seat. Betcha that's what happened."

Billy, who sat directly behind Fred, made as if to garrote him using the strings on Fred's sweatshirt. This got a knowing laugh out of the rest of the group.

All were Soprano fans, making them experts on the mob and mob's modus operandi. The fact that this program aired late on Sunday night when it was supposed to be well past bedtime for ninth graders and was hardly fourteen or fifteen-year old fare, didn't seem to be much of a restraint. The local parents would allow their children to watch anything the kids wanted to as long as they were quiet during it so as not to disturb the parents' TV viewing.

At this point in the conversation, the Student Council President broke in on the PA saying "Good Morning. All rise for the Pledge to the Flag."

By the time Jimmy was able to get his homeroom boys to their seats, their hats off, and calmed down, the daily recitation of The Pledge of Allegiance had gotten to the "under God" part. Aside from Jimmy and a few of the girls, no one noticed anyway.

****

Normally a county sheriff would not do a criminal investigation, much less lead one that appeared to be murder. Most counties had an undersheriff and deputies who were better qualified to head such an inquiry. The sheriff's job was to meet with the media, look serious, and say that everything that it was possible to do was being done and that he expected to bring the perpetrator or perpetrators to justice ASAP. That was what would happen if Palatine County had enough money in its budget: a) to have a full staff and b) to pay its deputies well enough to keep them on long term basis. As it was, Moe's six and a half deputies had barely had enough training to qualify for simple routine patrolling duty. With the exception of Bill Pierce—who had been a member of the now defunct Snyder's Corners police force and had just made a sideways move to the sheriff's office—all of the deputies ever hired by Palatine County came right out of some two-year college with an associate degree in criminal justice. Since they were new to the police business and opted for employment on Moe's force so quickly, they never had had the chance to explore the salary and benefits available in other areas. While in the process of joint training with other county forces, the Palatine Deputies soon learned about these better salaries from their counterparts from other areas of the state. At this point, which usually occurred just when they were beginning to be able to do some serious police work, they would quit Palatine County's force to take jobs that paid half again as much and with much better benefits. This meant Palatine County had a constant turnover of personnel in the sheriff's department and at any given time, the deputies who were on duty were neophytes.

Given the lack of personnel, it was fortunate that Palatine County did not have a jail to staff. A number of years ago, the country supervisors decided to replace the original jail which had been condemned by the state as unsanitary. However, the debate about a replacement caused such a hue and cry from the over-taxed voters, that the idea was shelved. This happened after the old jail had been torn down so it was never replaced. As a result, the sheriff's only lockup was a couple of holding cells attached to his office in Snyder's Corner's that he, or whoever was in the office doing dispatch work at the time, monitored. Usually the only occupants were DUIs that were sleeping it off or the occasional felon waiting for arraignment by the local justice of the peace. Once the charges were preferred and, unless bail was immediately posted, the prisoner was moved to a jail in an adjoining county. Palatine County then paid a daily boarding fee until the accused was either released or moved into the state penal system. This was cheaper for the county than actually operating its own jail and meant the sheriff's department mostly wrote appearance tickets rather than making arrests.

Luckily, aside from motor vehicular accidents, there was a relative lack of criminal activity in Palatine County so this worked out okay most of the time. By and large most what could be considered crime in the area was of the breaking and entering variety usually involving summer residences. Generally, it was not hard to pin down the perpetrators. If the B and E occurred during the weekends it was probably high school kids; if during the week, then high school dropouts were to blame. Given the small population, by the time he had been in office only a couple of months, most of the local criminals were well known to Moe. So by simply knowing where the crime occurred, the time that it occurred and what type of items were taken, he found it was fairly easy to trace down the possible suspects. Something he usually did himself.

Proving it was another matter. Since there was no way stolen property could be fenced in the county, most of the thefts consisted of consumables like money or booze. The exception was guns. These could be gotten rid of very easily at the guns shows in and around the county where they could be sold without background checks and with no questions asked. This made catching the perpetrator with the actual stolen property on his person difficult and decreased the chances of a conviction. Additionally, there was little chance of someone coming forth to turn anyone in to the authorities. Since all the locals were, in some way, related by birth or marriage, everyone was either someone's first or second cousin, and getting one thief to roll over on another was impossible. Additionally, if there was enough evidence for an arrest, chances were the thief was a relative of the Justice of the Peace so he or she usually got off with nothing more than a fine and warning. Ordinarily, Moe was just happy if some of the merchandize turned up so it could be returned.

The most serious and growing problem in the county was methamphetamine labs but this was not anything that Moe would touch. If the he or his deputies became aware of a meth lab in the area, they immediately turned the information over to the State Police and, while the Sheriff might send his people in to assist, they stayed fairly much out of the bust. After all, the chemicals used in these labs could be biologically hazardous, not to mention explosive, and, given how hard they were to replace, this kind of operation was not Moe's idea of a good way to cut down the size of his force.

In fact, it was while busting meth labs that Sidney Boyce and Moe had become acquainted. While working together on several investigations the two men had developed a mutual respect for each other's abilities and had become friends.

As far as murder was concerned, it was an infrequent occurrence in the county. The only case that had occurred during Moe's term had happened a year ago when two reclusive brothers out near Fierroville, in a dispute over who had the right to the last bottle of Genesee Cream Ale, went after each other with hunting knives. This was an easy crime to solve because when the deputies arrived, the murderer was sitting next to the victim drinking the last Genny. Whether due to his inebriated state or loss of blood, the killer was easily apprehended at the scene and there was not a lot of need for investigation. Once sober, the perpetrator admitted to the crime, pled guilty and was immediately hustled off to state prison thereby saving the county a considerable amount of money for housing.

This meant that in this murder case Moe was the best, and only one qualified to do this type of investigation so, sheriff or not, the job fell to him. He did not think the murder of Joey Scalani was going to be that easily solved. Somehow, Moe felt the key to the solution lay in finding an ATV that was missing some paint. Armed with this theory he went over to *Big Ed's Chain Saws, Snowmobile & ATV* located just outside Snyder's Corners.

****

In the late sixties and early seventies everybody and his brother had to have a snowmobile These marvels of engineering used a two-stroke engine to drive a movable belt that allowed the operator to travel at high rates of speed with a great deal of ear-shattering noise over snow. The problem was, shortly after their introduction to the public in Catskill Mountains, either due to Global Warming or just bad timing, the winters became milder and the amount of time there was enough snow on the ground to make the machine practical, diminished. In some areas, their owners adapted them to operate on grass and in mud, but in rugged, rock-strewn areas like Palatine County, there were not enough suitable places to operate them safely. The only alternative was to spend forty thousand dollars on an SUV or extended cab pickup and another seven thousand dollars on an enclosed trailer so one could haul their ten thousand dollar Arctic Cat or Ski-Doo to the Tughill Plateau or western Adirondacks. During most winters these places had a constant amount of snow and had created a winter tourist industry that catered to snowmobile enthusiasts. Otherwise, one's snowmobile just sat in the backyard and rusted away. This drop in the sale of units caused numerous businesses in places like Palatine County to go bankrupt and created a huge backlog of two-stroke engines at the manufacturers.

For those dealers like Big Ed who managed to stay in business, however, a new gadget came onto the market and save them. It did not take long for the Japanese companies to develop, and effectively market this new machine that harnessed these same engines to first three-wheeled and, later, four-wheeled, vehicles. This new "boy toy" evolved into the All Terrain Vehicle. With big balloon, low-pressure tires and 4-wheel drive, the ATV was an almost year-round, off-road vehicle. Now, not only was the lack of snow not a factor but other locales where it never snowed were now opened to sales. The fact that it was just as noisy as its predecessor did not seem to bother those who flocked to buy them. This may have, in fact, made them more desirable.

The first, three-wheel versions of these machines helped lower the gene pool of impulse buyers through attrition, as they proved unstable and too difficult to handle for all but the most experienced operators. However, by the 1980's gradual improvements in instruction and total elimination of the three-wheel models in response to the threat from federal legislation, which would have banned the importation of ATV's, convinced the buying public to get back into the market. This especially true in rural areas such as Palatine County where they proved to be especially useful.

For country landowners, farmers, loggers, rescue workers, and outdoor enthusiasts they provided an ideal vehicle to access fields and woods. The single biggest category of the latter group was deer hunters, who used ATV's to haul supplies into the woods and carcasses out. But they also caught on with the general public. Manufacturers made them in various sizes, from six-year old friendly 50 cc displacement models, to the big 90-plus cc monsters for adults. So now the whole family could ride. This led to the formation of "clubs" of several hundred members, who enjoyed motoring through field and forests while scaring the hell out of the wildlife and trampling down whatever could not get out of the way. While this did not do much for the environment and resulted in state, federal and private owners banning the machines from some areas, at least it passed for family entertainment. Although the amount of actual physical exercise was minimal and, usually, was limited to pushing a bogged down machine out of the mud, the kids were at least getting outside and away from video games.

Another result of these clubs was ATV meets, often call "runs". These events were gatherings of large numbers of ATV owning adults and children and could be anything from cross-country treks on a laid out course to motocross-type races. Whether trek or race, they pitted men and machines (or children and machines) against one another over a course that included on good days muddy wallows and better days water filled holes. The purpose of these get-togethers—besides to get as dirty as possible—was to show off the machines, the operator's driving skills and they or their father's, mechanical ability. This is because the American male, given access to a box of tools and a gasoline powered engine, is obligated to modify that engine so that any vehicle to which it can be attached will be louder and go faster. In the case of the ATV, by disassembling, adding new pipes, changing the carburetor jets and rebuilding it in ways they hinted at but refused to share, backyard mechanics made their machines to go faster than the manufacturers had ever intended. A whole industry grew up around the modification of the ATVs, furnishing add-on gadgets and manuals that would assist these mechanics in getting more power into and speed out of, their machines. Thus, these ATV meets ran the gamut from friendly rides to cutthroat competitions and, in some places, outdrew little league baseball and pewee soccer as weekend bonding between fathers and their kids. One of the telltale signs that a meet was in the area was that all the car washes would have signs posted "No ATVs" since washing the mud, grass and other debris off the machines would clog the drains in these facilities.

****

When it came to ATV runs, Palatine County was the hotbed of New York State and *Big Ed's Chain Saws, Snowmobile & ATV* was its headquarters. Moe knew this going in and was also pretty sure that if the green paint came from a locally owned machine, the owner bought it from Big Ed.

It was fortunate for Moe that Big Ed was very cooperative. There was a reason for this. Two winters ago, Moe had caught Big Ed's son, Eddie, in the act of breaking in to a "camp" out on Route 618. Fortunately, Moe apprehended Eddie before he did any damage and let him off with a warning before turning him over to his father. Big Ed was grateful, so when Moe came to him searching for ATV information, Big Ed was more than happy to be of assistance.

Given that Big Ed was one of the biggest Polaris dealers in the area, meant he had sold a large number of these machines. In the model years from 2003 through 2005, Big Ed had sold fifty-one green versions of the various Polaris models and, if the new owners were consistent with those in the rest of the state, they would have only licensed a few for on-road use. This meant that, had these machines just gone out of the door and were never licensed, it might have been a problem for Moe to track them down. However, given the readiness of the American public to refuse responsibility for any kind of an accident and sue the hell out of everyone with the least bit of connection with the product that injured them, there was a record of to whom every one of those machines was sold.

Four-wheeled ATV's, while they may look fairly easy to drive, do have unique handling properties. First, they are steered like a bicycle, which, because they have four, rather than two, wheels, causes them to have a rather wide turning radius. Second, most are sold with the balloon, low-pressure, off-road tires that grip turf well but make them extremely difficult to control on paved surfaces such as concrete or macadam. Finally, and most dangerously, they can be very unstable, especially when taking turns at high speeds, climbing steep grades or going side-hill, all of which require the rider to shift weight to maintain balance. All of these properties, sometimes in combination, have resulted in inexperienced drivers losing control and being thrown from the vehicle and/or having the vehicle land on them, occasionally with tragic results. Thus, ATV manufacturers, state law, and common sense required Big Ed and all ATV dealers to make sure that anyone buying an ATV knew how to operate it safely. To this end, all buyers were required to watch a DVD on the safety and handling and then take a driver education course. This course, as offered by Big Ed, consisted of doing a series of figure eights in the field behind his shop. Once the course was completed, the "trained" owner signed a release stating that he or she now understood the proper way to operate the new machine and would not let anyone else operate without similar training. It should be noted that not every buyer went through this procedure. Most adult males, rather than admit that they had never driven what they considered a child's toy, simply said that they already knew how to operate the machine and signed the release to that effect. Big Ed then filed these releases in case the owner/operator did something stupid and they, or their heirs, tried to sue the manufacturer and/or the dealer. Since these releases had the name, address and model of the machine sold, they made it possible to track down the owners easily.

With Big Ed's help, Moe was able to sort out the releases for those buyers of the green ATVs. Moe then asked Big Ed if he could borrow these releases for a few hours and, returning to the office, made photocopies of all fifty-one before returning them. Arranging them in order of their distance from Snyder's Corners, Moe figured it would take him about five days to go through the list at a rate of ten per day.

Now logic would suggest that the best course of action would be for Moe to check the owners closest to the crime scene. But Moe, being a veteran police officer, had long ago given up on logic when it came to chasing down clues. He knew that ninety-nine point nine percent of the time, the last place he looked would be where the case broke. Using this perverse form of logic then, he planned to start with those owners furthest from town and work back. He figured he would make out either way by either breaking the case early or, if later, breaking it closer to home. Besides, he had a feeling that the person he was looking for was not going anyplace.

Reluctantly he then decided: *To hell with the board of supervisors, I'll keep Bill Pierce on as a full-time deputy for at least another week to cover for me.*

Chapter 5

After a week of watching the same movie five times a day, Phyllis Nielsen was over the edge of boredom and into ennui. By the third showing of *Sense and Sensibility* on Friday afternoon, she was quite ready for something else, anything else. After starting the movie for the fifth period class and noting how most of the students had carefully arranged their backpacks as pillows—something she tried to discourage the first day, but now simply let go in admiration of the students' ingenuity—she went to the desk in the back of the room.

This was not what she had in mind when she went into teaching. Her goals had been to extend the knowledge of her students, pique their curiosity and enable them to become better citizens who were more useful to themselves and society. She loved the challenge of doing this and, had it not been for the unfortunate encounter with that cad of an elementary principal, she very well would still have been in Minnesota. She possessed, after all, those qualities that would make a good teacher; she had intelligence, compassion, love of learning and empathy for children and their problems. Even the little contact she had had with students while at her previous job was rewarding to both her and the children.

This isn't teaching, she thought, *it's babysitting and, at fifty-five dollars a day, I'm being way too underpaid for that kind of a job.*

Reaching the desk, she turned on the *Itty Bitty Reading Light* that she found in the upper, middle drawer. Apparently, Meyers kept it there so, while his students were either watching the movie or napping, he could read. Phyllis had neglected to bring anything to read today so, since she owed her parents a letter, she figured to catch up on her correspondence. However, she also had forgotten to bring any stationery.

No problem, she thought, *surely as an English teacher, Meyers should have paper in his desk.*

She commenced opening drawers looking for some. After empty drawer after empty drawer, she finally found what appeared to be blank sheets of paper in the lower right-hand drawer but when she took them out, she realized that there was printing on the reverse side. Turning a sheet over, she found that the heading read "**English-8 Competency Examination, June 18, 2006**". Under this heading were the words "**Answer Sheet**". What was unusual about this sheet was that all the answers—multiple-choice, which required filling in the circles with a number two-pencil, and blanks for writing one-word answers—had been completely filled in. Except for the addition of a student's name, each answer sheet was ready for scoring. Furthermore, all of the five sheets she held in her hand were exactly alike, an original, which was on top, and four excellent photocopies. These copies were so good, in fact, that had she not had the original, done in red ink rather that the black of the copies, she would have not known they were copies. Phyllis found herself mildly interested in why Meyers kept these in his lower drawer, but not being familiar with New York examination policy, she returned them and promptly dismissed them from her mind.

She then dug through the mass of papers strewn about on the desk's top until she found a partially used one containing a directive regarding the monitoring student restrooms to prevent smoking. Since the writing took up less than half a page, by creasing and carefully tearing it over the edge of the desk, she was able to get a good two-thirds of a sheet of usable paper.

Picking up her pen, she began, *"Dear Mom and Dad,..."*

****

What Phyllis Nielsen did not know was that the answer sheet she had just seen was for the latest in an evolutionary process that was over one-hundred-forty years in the making. On July 27, 1864, the Board of Regents of New York State had instituted a statewide preliminary examination; given to all eighth grade students to assure they were competent enough to advance to the next level of academics or had successfully completed their education. In addition to its use as an exit exam, this test would allow the Board of Regents to monitor of how well each of the individual schools in the state were educating their students and would also act as a basis for allocation of funds. Gradually this "preliminary" examination went from a single test to a battery of tests in English, Mathematics, Civics, Social Studies and Science. These exams were given to eighth grade students in June of each year—with make-up exams in January and August. If a student failed two or more, especially the Math, Civics and English exams, it often meant he or she did not get out of the eighth grade. On the other hand, passing all these exams was considered such an educational accomplishment that it conferred full citizenship on the student with all the rights and privileges thereof. Therefore a student who passed all five was free, if he or she so choose, to leave the educational system at the end of eighth grade. With jobs available to children at this age, many of them elected to do this.

The first test was given in November of 1865 and by 1876 the Board of Regents was so happy with the results that they expanded the testing procedure to secondary schools throughout the state. Within two years, high school students were able to take some forty-two exams in every area of academics including Virgil's Aeneid books 1-2. (If the student passed this, the follow year they could take the exam for Virgil's Aeneid books 3 -6.) Over the next hundred years the state added and dropped examinations in a variety of courses but, rest assured, at one time or another, they tested just about everything and anything that could have been taught including Home Economics and Agriculture. Interestingly, there was one notable exception. This kind of scrutiny never applied to Physical Education. Collectively, these exams became known as "Regents Examinations" or simply "Regents".

Gradually a system evolved for the creation of these tests as well as their security. A bank of questions for each subject's exam was created by a group of educators based on the State's syllabus for the particular course. They were then trial tested in a select group of schools, evaluated for difficulty based on these trials and, finally, used. Step by step a format was devised for each type of examination and, often, the questions used repeated in different forms or, in the case of mathematics subjects, using the same questions with different numbers. Thus, while difficulty might have varied, most of the tests were fair and a good evaluation of what was going on in the state's schools.

For the first eighty years of their existence, these exams had their place in the educational system. They were an ideal way to measure a student's achievement against not only his or her peers throughout the state but as a good indication of the student's knowledge of the particular subject. Often students, especially WWII vets that dropped out prior to graduation, used the exams to gain credit for courses without ever having taken them. Lacking other types of tests, colleges would use good Regents grades as criteria for acceptance. Aside from the eighth grade exams, students could opt out of taking the exams and choose to get local credit for the courses with no stigma attached to either not taking the exams or to failing them.

That changed in the late 1950's when the public became concerned about the growing need for advanced education beyond high school. Also the SAT exams were gaining national prominence so that New York State students and schools were now compared, not only with each other, but nationally. Sometimes, especially when the student took the SAT's without taking the Regents as well, these comparisons were less than stellar. Suddenly there was pressure on all students to take and pass Regents, on the teachers to get their students through them, and on the districts to show good results. This kind of pressure was bound to cause some fallout. The greatest of this was in the way many teachers taught those courses where Regents were required.

First, it created a cottage industry in New York State whereby review books and study guides, aimed specifically at these exams and including collections of the most recent Regents' questions, were made available. Second, those teachers who felt especially pressured to have good Regents results now began using these review books as their primary text and taught strictly for the exams. Instead of teaching the subject, these teachers required their students to memorize material and test questions, hoping that these questions and/or answers would be repeated on the exams. Thus, the students memorized questions and answers that often made little sense and which they promptly forgot once the test was over. This meant the tests results measured not knowledge but memorization skills and the ability to take tests.

As far as the parents, administrators and school boards of education were concerned, this made no difference. These groups based their evaluation of a teacher solely on how many students that teacher "got through" the Regents, rather than how well the students learned the subject. Often, if a teacher had too many failures, especially if they were the sons or daughters of influential parents, the teacher would end up seeking employment elsewhere.

Things fairly much muddled along like this until the late 1960's when there was a growing feeling that the inmates should be running the institution and the teachers and their students were in a better position than some bureaucrat in Albany to decide what should be taught in the individual schools. At the same time, some academics felt there was too much pressure placed on students with, correspondingly, too many tests given. This resulted, first, in 1960, with the complete discontinuation of the eighth grade exams. In addition, the number of secondary versions was cut to a basic twenty-two—three consecutive in mathematics, a choice of one of six languages(including Latin), four in science, six in business subjects, and one each in English, World and American History. Additionally, most of these were dummied down to make them easier to pass. Teachers, freed from teaching to the exams, now could offer alternative courses in such things as Women's Studies, alternative arithmetic, poetry, government studies, and general science.

Then in the 1980's the pendulum, as it does in education, swung the other way. Parents, academics, educators, and industrial leaders awoke to the fact that students coming out of colleges and secondary schools, while learning a lot of stuff, did not know what parents, academics, educators and industrial leaders thought they should know.

(The kids did not know the states and their capitols, for God sake!) It did not take long for politicians to jump on this bandwagon and for the word "accountability" to enter the educational lexicon. Moreover, what better way to check for the "accountability" but tests? This meant lots of tests and, for the first time in over twenty years, they reinvaded the lower levels. Under the new policy, tests were to be administrated in the fourth, sixth, and eighth grades with no opting out. Soon a whole new group of teachers found they no longer had the time to teach their students how to get along with each other, take field trips to learn about their heritage and culture, learn to enjoy reading for reading's sake, or simply have the freedom to think. The teachers had tests to dictate what they had to teach.

When the *Elementary and Secondary Education Act of 2001* (also known as the "No Child Left Behind Act") was signed into law by President George W. Bush, New York State was ready. The Board of Regents already had the tests and a statewide system in place to distribute them. This was going to make it easy to monitor results and allocate state and now, federal funds.

Security measures to prevent the tests from being previewed or the results tampered with also had evolved over the years. These new tests, like all Regents, are sent via a common carrier to each district in locked, steel boxes for which only the school's principal had the key. Thus secured, no one in the district sees them until the appointed day and hour the test is to be given. So strict is this security that, should a school be unable to administer an exam on the appointed day and hour due to such catastrophes as a water main break or snow day, the students are out of luck and have to wait for the next series of exams. As a further precaution and until the conclusion of the test; the answers are locked in the same box and withheld from the teachers. This was to prevent the teachers from helping the students although this seemed to ignore the fact that most teachers were capable of answering the questions without help.

The only flaw in the procedure is, rather than go through the expense of hiring an outside agency to correct the tests, that the actual classroom teacher does the grading of his or her own student's exams. To minimize the possibility that this could result in cheating, the state covers themselves in two ways. First, those teachers that monitor and/ or grade the exams are required to sign a post-test affidavit, under penalty of perjury and loss of their teaching license, to the effect that they have not helped students answer the exam nor have they altered answers or scores on it. Second, the tests, once graded, are returned to the secure steel box, locked up and sent back to the state for a possible regrading as a check on the teacher's integrity.

What Phyllis saw in the bottom drawer was an attempt by Milt Meyers to circumvent these safeguards.

****

Born and raised in Southern California, Milt Meyers was the worst kind California Kid in that while he was highly intelligent, he was laid back to the point of being lazy. This caused him, at an early age, to discover that the best way to avoid any kind of work was to be seen holding some sort of printed matter. By giving the appearance of being engrossed in a book, he was, by and large, ignored by his peers, teachers, parents and, later in life, employers. This was not entirely a wasted time. Having a photographic memory, he absorbed much from his reading and, consequently, did well in those subjects in school such as English and History, where reading, writing and spelling were the basic requirements but poorly in those where actual work and thinking were required, like Math and Science. By carefully avoiding the latter, he managed to graduate from high school in the upper third of his class and be accepted at the University of California at Long Beach with little problem. Majoring in English with a minor in History, he had little trouble maintaining a high enough GPA to move directly from undergrad to graduate school and, thus, avoid having to find immediate employment. It was while working on his master's degree that he also added enough graduate courses in Education to become qualified as a high school English teacher.

Since his graduate school years coincided with the tail end the Vietnam War and because of an unfavorable Selective Service Number, it appeared that he might be drafted so he joined the California National

Guard. As luck would have it, the unit he joined was a motorized one and Milt was taught to drive their big rigs. Driving a semi for the military was ideal for Milt as all he was required to do was to move a load of something from one place to another—loading and unloading being the job of someone else while he read. Since this driving could be done while sitting in one position for long periods of time it fit his life style to a tee. So while Milt took a series of high school English teaching jobs—never managing to stay for more than a year or two at any one—he continued as a part-time warrior. Eventually he might even have made it a career had it not been for the fact that Saddam Hussein decided to invade Kuwait.

This meant that the rumors Jimmy and the rest of the staff had heard about Milt Meyers and his military service were totally false. Milt neither had served in the Vietnam War nor was ever in the Special Services. Rather he was a pfc, in the California Nation Guard, who had been called up during the first Gulf War and served as a driver in a motor pool out of Kuwait City. It was here that Milt served under and was befriended by Captain Everett Shay; who was later to become the CSO of the Kaaterskill Central School. Captain Shay was Meyers' commanding officer and because they shared a common civilian vocation, Shay often rode shotgun with Milt when he delivered gasoline to the front lines.

During one such trip—Milt's last as it turned out— they were caught in a sandstorm and because of the confusion, their convoy was mistaken for a group of retreating Iraqi vehicles and fired on by a squad of Bradley Armored Vehicles. One of the shells penetrated the tanker Milt was driving causing it to explode with terrifying result. Fortunately both he and Shay had abandoned the vehicle when it first came under attack and survived the inferno by diving into a ditch and covering themselves with sand. This incident did have, however, a lasting effect on Milt. Diagnosed as suffering from post-traumatic stress disorder (PTSD); he was immediately sent home. After he returned to civilian life, for all intents and purposes, Milt seemed normal and managed to keep incidents of his PTSD under control. However there were occasional relapses when Milt would have hallucinations, curl up in a fetal position, attempt to dig himself into imaginary sand and sob uncontrollably. According to the army psychologist, the triggering mechanism for these episodes was most likely extreme stress.

Upon being discharged from the Veteran's hospital and, because he was unable to continue in the military, Milt sought out his former commanding officer for help. By this time Everett Shay had become CSO of the KCS and, in an unusual moment of compassion, Everett offered his former military colleague a position. Fortunately, for the most part, the PTSD did not interfere with Milt's teaching. He was able, because of his teaching methods, to avoid stress throughout most of the school year but, recently, at the beginning of school each fall apparently due to the stress of actually returning to work, he came under enough pressure to trigger brief psychotic episodes.

Fortunately, Shay knew of his colleague's problem and because they had shared this same experience, Shay saw to it that the faculty, members of the support staff and, most importantly, the board of education, did not find out about Milt's problem. To cover this, he and Milt had devised a ruse by which Milt would take the two weeks he needed to recover at a Veteran's facility and Shay would give him leave of absence for military service. This tiny lie, abetted by the rumors they carefully spread about Milt's military service, allowed Milt to retain his accumulative sick leave days and, because Shay was the only one who knew the truth, prevented any report of his problem from appearing in Milt's teaching file where it would be open to the public. Therefore, while Phyllis Nielsen was being bored to death watching Jane Austin novels that had been made into movies, Milt was having his head shrunk.

****

"We've got to stop meeting like this."

Phyllis turned to see Jimmy Kalid smiling at her. It was the fifth time this week they had come out of school at the same time. "Seems you and I are leaving together every day."

"Yeah, seems that way. How's the movie business going?" Jimmy was smiling.

"Terrible, I've never been so bored in my life, Jane Austin all week. I haven't seen next week's plans. But I'm willing to bet, with my luck, Monday's movie will be *Wuthering Heights*. My guess would be that Emily Bronte is next up. Must be he wants to get all this stuff out of the way before he gets back."

"Oh wow, *Wuthering Heights*, I hope it is the 1938 version with Laurence Olivier rather than the 71 version with Timothy Dalton."

"God, I don't really care, with five showings a day, they will be equally bad. I wonder how the kids manage to put up with it."

"Kids are pretty adaptable. I imagine they just put their brains on hold for the period or think about what most adolescents think about."

"And that would be?"

"Sex"

It was Phyllis' turn to smile. "You're probably right."

Jimmy could not help but notice that when Phyllis smiled her whole face lit up. She was a beautiful young woman in spite of the fact she seemed to be going out of her way to hide it. The lack of make-up, her hair up in a bun and that damn green dress that she seemed to wear every day was not helping. In Jimmy's imagination, that dress hid a nice figure.

Stop it! , he thought, *you hardly know the girl and you're undressing her.*

While in this thought, he caught himself staring at her. It impressed him that rather than self-consciously looking away as many girls would do when she was being checked out, Phyllis returned his look and her eyes held his gaze. He found himself trying to avoid looking below her neck.

"Say, a bunch of us go over to the Snyder's Corners Tavern every Friday after school for a few drinks. How would you like to join us? I had to spend two hours in the cold watching a field hockey game last night, yesterday I also missed lunch because I had two kids in for detention and I still have seven AP essays to grade before Monday." He held up a four-inch thick folder which was stuffed with papers. "I need someplace warm and dry tonight to unwind."

"I don't know, first I'm not much of a drinker and second I'm a little low on funds right now."

"Forget the money, the treat's on me. It's the best I could do to help you come down from all that Austin. Besides you'll get a chance to meet some of the less weird members of the faculty. In fact, if you're hungry, they make the best burgers in town, my treat too"

"Ok, I guess one drink wouldn't hurt." She was ignoring his dinner invitation, if that was what it was. "Maybe it will help steel me for Heathcliff."

"That's the idea. If you don't know where The Tavern is, you can follow me."

"Ok, you lead." Phyllis knew where the local pub was, having passed it a number of times on her trips around town but she would let Jimmy think he was performing a service. "I do need to stop at the Post Office on the way to mail a letter."

"No problem, the Post Office is right across the street from The Tavern."

****

Phyllis came in a couple of minutes after Jimmy and once her eyes got used to the dimness of the light in the bar, she spotted him sitting at its far end. She also recognized a few of the teachers gathered around the end of the bar: Tim Post, the high school math teacher, Mary Phillips, who taught girls' phys ed, Susan Curry, the art teacher and Mike Case, whose size made him easy to distinguish even in the semidarkness. There were others with them that she did not know: a couple of whom seemed young enough to be students themselves. When she joined the group, Jimmy introduced her to everyone as well as everyone to her. It turned out that a few were KCS graduates that hung around with their old teachers.

She immediately forgot most of the names.

Some place in Phyllis Nielsen's Danish heritage there was a line of lousy drinkers; a trait that had been passed along to her. Whether it was simply lack of practice or the defective genes, made no difference: one beer, she became talkative; two, she got giddy; on the third, she became an exhibitionist; and, for some unknown reason, with the fourth one, she lost her inhibitions completely and, despite her Midwest Lutheran upbringing and if conditions were right, became an uncontrollable sexpot. Unconsciously she realized she now must have finished her third beer because she was mindlessly talking with Susan about the Impressionist Period of Art, something she did not know a damn thing about—and Susan was agreeing with her.

****

"Hey, I promised you a burger. Ready?" Jimmy's voice was coming from somewhere beyond the scope of her eyesight.

"I'd better." She said, "Or I'll topple over any minute."

"OK." He took her hand and led her to a booth in the dining room. He also brought along her beer from the bar.

They sat on opposite sides of the last booth in the row. When the waitress finally made an appearance, they both ordered burgers with a side of fries, she asking specifically that her burger be well-done. Jimmy ordered another round of beer. Phyllis, who was really having a good time for the first time since the start of that dinner back in Minneapolis, did not object.

By the time they polished off their meals, which, Jimmy could not help but notice, Phyllis had relished, they were midway through the next beer. This was Phyllis' fourth.

"So, what do you think of Snyder's Corners?" Jimmy was attempting to make conversation.

"I love it. I'm not used to the hills. Where I come from it's either rolling knolls or flat as a pancake. Also, the changing of the seasons is so beautiful too. I especially love the colorful leaves." As Phyllis spoke and having decided Jimmy wasn't half bad in a dark kind of way, she had slipped off her right shoe and, reaching her foot under the table, was working her toes up along the inside of his thigh. It had, she remember, been a long time since she had had any sex.

"I noticed from your plates that you were from Minnesota, Land of 10,000 Lakes." *What in hell was this woman doing?* Jimmy wondered. "They will get better too. The leaves, I mean." He was beginning to squirm, not quite sure what her actions meant.

Granted he found her interesting and her Minnesota accent, with the lilting hint of Scandinavian overtones was pleasing to his ear, especially after years of down-state New York hard a's. But this was a first date, if it was a date, and he wasn't ready for the foot on his inner thigh thing.

"Yup good old Minnesota." She said and before Jimmy could stop her, Phyllis had climbed up on the table and began to sing.

"'Minnesota, hats off to thee,
To our colors true we shall ever be,
Firm and strong, united are we,
Rah ,Rah, Rah, Ski-U- Mah,
Rah , Rah, Rah, Rah
Rah for the U of M'.
Go Gophers!"

Jimmy was definitely not ready for that. Then it occurred to him, *Oh hell, she's drunk.*

"Tell you what." Jimmy, like everyone else's in the room, had his head tilted upward so he could watch the show, "It looks like it's time we got you out of here and home. I'll take you in your car and get Tim to follow me to bring me back. Sound ok with you?"

He rose for the booth and offer her is hand. She ignored it.

"Okey dokey." Phyllis said and then leaned toward where Jimmy was standing, making her body rigid, she toppled toward him like a just felled tree. Had Jimmy known Phyllis had learned gymnastics while a cheerleader at Minnesota Valley Lutheran High in New Ulm, Minnesota, he might have been ready for what happened next. He did not. So he stood and reached up with both arms to catcher her. She, however, knew exactly what she was doing, and was under complete control. Doing a perfectly executed dismount, she landed between his outstretched arms, her arms around his neck and her head on his shoulder. Her feet still extended straight back onto the table. All he had to do was stagger slightly backward away from the table and she was on her feet, upright and holding him around the neck. It was a perfect dismount and her coach at MVLHS would have been proud— all she left off was the "Go Chargers!!" cheer at the end.

"Ta Da!" She said and in this final dismount position, her lips were right next to Jimmy's right ear. "Take me home to bed." She whispered, blowing in to his ear.

Jimmy did not acknowledge the invitation. Rather he helped her find her shoes and then, holding her upright, as she now seemed a bit unsteady, he guided her out to her car. It was not hard to locate it, since it was the only one with Minnesota plates in the parking lot. Settling her into the passenger side, he went back inside to explain to Tim why he had to follow him. He also ignored Mike Case's leer.

By the time he got back to her car, Phyllis had her keys out. "Know were I live?" she inquired.

"No, but I expect you'll be able to help me." Jimmy started the car and checked in the mirror to be sure Tim had lined up behind him.

As foggy as Phyllis' brain was, it had only derailed her inhibitions, not her sense of direction. She was able to guide Jimmy to her trailer with ease. As they were pulling down the driveway, she leaned over and stuck her tongue into his ear. "Don't you find me sexy?"

Honestly Jimmy answered "Yes, but you're drunk I don't want to take advantage of that."

"You don't like me!" She was now clinging to him. "Come in with me?"

Jimmy, as a male, one hundred percent, red-blood American of Middle Eastern heritage, was finding it difficult to turn down this kind of invitation. Especially one offered when the inviter's tongue was in the invitee's ear while was pressing her breasts against his chest simultaneously exploring his crotch. This was going to prove to be a no-brainer.

Jimmy stopped the car and, without hesitating lest he change his mind, went back to tell Tim to go on without him, Phyllis would take him back to the Jeep later. Tim gave him a goofy, shit-assed grin and backed out of the driveway to the road. Meanwhile, she had removed the keys from the ignition, got out of the car and staggered up the steps to open the door.

Jimmy stood and watched the taillights of Tim's car disappeared back toward town before going up the steps to Phyllis' mobile home.

When he came in the door, Phyllis was standing in the middle of her living room, the green dress in a heap on the floor. In an instant, Jimmy saw that his imagination had been right; she did have a hell of a figure. The bra went on top of the dress and before Jimmy could take another step, he was assured that, *Yes, Phyllis Nielsen was a natural blond.*

There was one other thing about Phyllis' inherited intolerance of alcohol. When the last of the fourth beer hit her brain, she would invariably pass out. Tonight this would happen the second after her panties hit the floor.

Later when he had a chance to reflect, Jimmy was not sure what followed was because he was a true gentleman or just because Phyllis passed out. At any rate, this time she was not under control as she fell and he caught her just before she landed face first on the floor. Taking a quick look around to get his bearings, he located the bedroom and carried her into it. Shooing the cat off the bed, he pulled down the comforter, blankets, top sheet and carefully placed her naked body in the middle of the bed. He covered her. By the time he had her fully covered, she had begun to snore softly. He watched her sleep for just a minute, admiring the smile on her face, and then returned to the main room. Not wanting to spend the night, he found her car keys under the pile of her discarded clothes and after carefully locked her door, got in to her car and drove home. He would return the car tomorrow.

****

Tony and Clarissa Torrelli were devastated when a hysterical Isabel called to tell them that Joey had been found dead in a field in upstate New York. After the funeral on Friday afternoon, the Torrelli's had gone to the Scalani's but no amount of condolences or booze could take the hurt away. To top it off, Tony became obsessed with the idea that whoever killed Joey was trying, in someway, to get back at him. All Friday night he tossed and turned, unable to think who in his past would have had a vendetta against him.

There would have been the guy he had tried to whack, but the intended victim had ended up in the Federal Witness Program and, presumably, would be happy to be out of circulation. Besides, the guy never did know who it was that was supposed to shoot him any way. As far as the politicians and the mob were concerned, Tony "borrowed" money from them that would never be missed. It had been a simple, foolproof plan, Tony just told the mob that the politician's price was higher than it actually was and skimmed the difference. Since he was sure the two groups would never get together to compare notes, Tony had managed to earn a nice bonus on every deal. No, there was no way either group could have figured it out and come for Tony. He was sure of it. But still....

By Saturday morning, this obsession had reached the point where Tony decided he had to check out who was responsible for his nephew's death. He told Clarissa nothing of his plans but just said he was going away for a few days and, since this was something he often did in his previous life in the mob, she thought nothing of it. He packed his overnight bag and called a car rental agency. They said they would not have the make or model of vehicle he requested ready for him until the next afternoon so he opted to wait for another day. After all, he was not in a hurry since he had not formulated a plan. Basically he figured he would start at his nephew's apartment in Albany and if he could not find anything there would go to the hick town in the Catskills where Joey's body had been found. Somehow, Tony felt whoever was responsible was not going anyplace.

****

Like most people who spend their lives in New York City and the surrounding suburbs, Tony never owned a car. Anyone knowledgeable with the NYC mass transit system could get anywhere in The City, Long Island or upper Jersey with little problem and at minimum cost by taking the bus and/or subway. If a person really had to get someplace in a hurry, there were always taxis, which rarely overcharged native New Yorkers. Besides, owning a car in NYC meant you had to find a place to park it which was either expensive, impossible, or both.

Whenever the Torrelli's needed to go on a trip of any kind, they simply rented a car, preferably a big one, and went. Unlike many city dwellers, Tony had long ago gotten his New York State driver's license, mainly because his early work for the mob often required him to drive—he was also required not to remember who went on the trip and who didn't come back.

There was one problem however, since Tony had changed jobs, he had been so busy that he and Clarissa had had no time for a trip for several years. Because of this, it had been a while since Tony had used his driver's license and, therefore, he had failed to notice it had expired on his birthday five years ago.

Normally this kind of thing is hard to miss since the State Department of Motor Vehicles sends out reminders prior to one's license expiration. Consequently, a reminder had been sent to Tony six months before his was to expire which would have given him ample time to renew. However, when the clerk at the post office in Albany tried to feed too many envelopes through the canceling machine at one time, the one containing Tony's renewal notice had jammed in the machinery. When the repairman found it, he handed it back to the clerk who, being in a rush and only semiliterate, saw *Jamaica* in the address and placed it in the bag bound for the West Indian island. Had it arrived there, the Jamaican postal authorities would have probably laughed their asses off and returned the letter to the States. Unfortunately, the winds from Hurricane Eloise blew the transport plane carrying that particular bag of mail off course and into Cuban airspace. Thinking it was the leading edge of an invasion of Cuban expatriates from Florida; the Cuban air force scrambled and forced the plane down into the Caribbean. Rescued, the pilot was returned to the United States—with apologies from Castro himself—but the cargo was lost. Consequently, Tony never received the reminder that he needed to renew his license and unknowingly he had let it lapse.

An alert clerk at the rental agency would probably have picked this up, except that Juan Rodriquez, the young man who waited on Tony at the agency, was not that competent. Having just come back to the counter after his morning break, Juan had hit not only on the girl at the car returns counter but taken one on a joint of Canada's finest. The buzz that he received from both encounters had scrambled his brain just enough so that when he looked at Tony's driver's license he mistakenly reversed the digits of the month and year on the expiration date. Instead of seeing the date as 10-09-01, he saw it as 01-09-10 so, as far as Juan was concerned, Tony was good for another five years. The fact that, had Juan's date been correct, it would have been only good for less than four years was not import to Juan as arithmetic not one of his strong suits. What was important was that Juan foggy brain misfired.

Therefore, on a Sunday morning of October 2006, as Tony Torrelli headed his rental Lincoln Continental across the Tappan Zee Bridge on his way to Albany with his cell phone in his pocket and a .38 caliber revolver tucked safely under the seat, he was driving illegally.

****

The ringing of the phone awoke Jimmy. Rolling over, he reached for it.

"You know anything about my missing car?" Although Phyllis did not have his phone number, it was no surprise that she was able to find it. Jimmy, as were all the KCS teachers, was listed in the phone book.

"Yeah, I didn't want to walk home from your place. It's a long way on a Friday night."

"Are you going to bring it back?"

"Of course, when do you need it?" He looked at the bedside clock; it was eight.

"I'd like it today."

"OK, just as soon as I get some breakfast, I'll bring it over." Jimmy was sure there were some orange juice and a stale donut around some place.

"If you bring it back now, I'll fix you breakfast."

"Sounds like a plan. See you in about fifteen minutes or so." Jimmy hung up went in to shower and shave, not sure why he was doing this on a nonschool morning.

Phyllis was still in her bathrobe when she answered the door. As per normal, she had no makeup on but, for a change, her hair was down. This was the first time Jimmy had seen it that way, and he liked it. He noticed too that it was still damp; apparently, she had taken a shower as well.

"Come on in, coffee's ready. How do you like your eggs?"

"Over easy, thanks. Here are the car keys. I'll need a ride back to the Tavern to get my car, by the way."

"Put them on the table." She waved the spatula she was holding in the direction of the kitchen table. "I take you after breakfast. For now, help yourself to the coffee and have a seat. I hope you like your coffee strong—Midwestern roots, you know."

Jimmy poured himself a cup of coffee and took a sip. It was strong. He found himself searching for cream and sugar. Finding it, he added enough to sweeten and lighten what was in his cup. He sat down at the kitchen table.

"Dig in." Phyllis slid him a plate with two eggs, over easy, and two slices of toast. She had done the eggs perfectly.

Neither of them talked while they ate and it was not until she was placing the dishes in the sink that Phyllis broke the silence.

"How did I get undressed and into bed last night?"

"Well, you sort of undressed yourself." Jimmy smiled at the thought, "I put you in bed."

"Did we?" she made a gesture with her thumb and pinkie.

"Nope, I was a perfect gentleman. As soon as I was sure you were asleep, I left."

"Wow, you are a gentleman, Jimmy Kalid."

"My momma brought me up to respect womankind. Besides, you were so far gone you wouldn't have enjoyed it anyway."

Phyllis just laughed. "More coffee?" She came around the table with the pot.

"Sure." As she leaned over him to pour it in the cup, Jimmy caught the scent of her bath soap.

"You're a real gentleman, Jimmy Kalid." She said it again and leaned down to kiss him on the lips. "But you don't have to be one now."

At this point, Jimmy realized three things: She was not drunk. The kiss she just gave him was not meant for any gentleman. And, Phyllis Nielsen had nothing on under the bathrobe.

This time it was she who shooed the cat off the bed.

The AP essays were not going to get graded until real late on Sunday night.

Chapter 6

On the Wednesday morning before Joey Scalani became the "late" Joey Scalani, he was working at his desk in his cubical of the State Education Building in Albany. There were just two steps in the job he performed on the stack of June 2006, *English-8 Competency Examination, Answer Sheet* packets on his desk. The first step, which he had already finished, was to take the packets of answer sheets that came in from each school system in the state and organize them in alphabetical order. This was necessary so that the packets received could be compared with an alphabetized list of schools in the state to be sure all schools had sent in their results. The second step, which he had nearly half completed, was to go back, remove the individual answer sheets from each school's packet and arrange them in numerical order according to marks received by the students. Once he had completed this job— which pretty much left him free until the next testing period—he sent the packets to another cubical where another member of the division would key the school's name and marks into a computer.

The computer would, ultimately, total all the scores, average them and then compare the results for each individual school to this overall state result. This done, the school would receive a "mark" based on the number of students who passed. (Also, but less important except for publicity purposes, the school would be compared with schools in the rest of the state.) That "mark" would determine how well the school system was teaching, in this case, English. A poor "mark" and the school would receive a strongly worded reprimand from the State Educational Department. Too many years of poor "marks", coupled with failure to show yearly improvement in scores, could result in designating the school as "failing". While, ordinarily a "failing" school would be given ample time to improve, under the worst case scenario it could mean that the Commissioner of Education could order the school be taken over and administrated by the State Education Department. In these extreme cases the parents in the district could be given the option of removing their children from the school and sending them elsewhere—presumably to a nonfailing school—at their home district's expense. Since the amount of state aid a school received was dependent on the school's average daily attendance this latter option, the removal of a number of students, would lower the total funding for the district. In a double whammy, the U.S. Department of Education could note the state's action, step in and reduce what little funding the district received through the No Child Left Behind laws. It, therefore, behooved a school to do well on these tests since reduction of state and federal funding meant the local district had to increase the real estate tax levy to make up for the lost funds—not to mention the added transportation costs to transport students to another district.

This could set off a chain reaction of sorts that would be disastrous for a school district. Since taxpayers, most of whom where already upset about increasing real property tax as well as state and federal income taxes, voted on the school district's budget. Given this one opportunity to have a say in how much they were taxed, they would often take out their frustrations by voting against a budget as a protest against all taxes. Under normal circumstances, there was an enough yearly increase in state and federal aid that an adept school board managed to do enough of a fast shuffle with numbers, equalization rates and percentages to minimize any tax increase. These prevented the voting public from getting too angry or organized well enough to defeat a budget. However, should there be a loss of state and federal aid it would mean a substantial increase in property tax, which would become a rallying point around which diverse groups could better organize against the budget and defeat it. With a defeated budget there would be monetary cuts which would mean reduced programs.

When forced to cut the budget, the school board's first move would be to reduce staff. If this was not enough then they would follow it by doing away with programs hidden away inside the buildings like art, music, and special education. Finally, if more reduction was needed there was also a real chance that extracurricular activities would be affected. This meant curtailing or, under the worst case, completely shutting down interscholastic sports. This, in turn, had a profound effect on those alumni and parents who lived vicariously through either their high school team and/or children/players. In addition, the parents of athletes often pointed out that the loss of interscholastic games could well mean their star player would miss out on an athletic scholarship to college. Not only could it mean the child might not get into a college at all but, assuming he or she did, there would be added college expenses for the parents. Worse still, the chance to play at the intercollegiate level would certainly short-circuit their child's chance at a pro career.

The end result could be a large group of very unhappy people who directed this anger at the school and those in charge of it. School boards of education as well as their Chief School Officers do not like large groups of angry people so they do their utmost to avoid this kind of situation.

Joey's job then, while a boring one, was important to the financial well-being of the state's school districts making Joey an important cog in the financial machinery of the New York State public education.

****

The packets came to Joey wrapped in a blue cover sheet that had the name of the test, the name of the school, an alphabetized list of every student whose answer sheet was in the packet and, next to the name, in a separate column, the student's score on the test. The student's passing scores were in either blue or black ink while the failing ones were in red. Down at the bottom of the page of this cover sheet were the total number of students taking the exam, the number passing and number failing. Joey usually ignored these totals since, as a rule they were wrong. Generally, it was an honest mistake; the person correlating the scores had simply miscounted. However, sometimes, there seemed to be a definite attempt on the part of the person submitting the results to mislead the state into thinking a greater percent of students passed than actually did. Often when the number passing was added to the number failing, it did not equal the total taking the test thus skewing the percentages. Since Joey ignored these numbers anyway, it made little difference and was not worth his time to check what the person reporting the scores had written. His primary concern was with the grades on the answer sheets themselves.

The next step in Joey's job consisted of removing the answer sheets and restacking them in grade-numerical order. As he did this, he gave a cursory check to make sure that each of school supplied "booklets" with the students' Part 2 subjective answers enclosed the corresponding state supplied Part 1 objective answer sheet. The Part 1 answers counted for sixty percent of the student's score while Part 2 accounted for the rest and it was important that both parts were there and together in case there was any discrepancy in the total score. (This most often happened because the person giving the grade totaled wrong, something more apt to occur on the mathematics exam than the English.)

Joey had finished the J schools Tuesday afternoon and was just starting on the K's that morning. The first school in the list was Kaaterskill Central School.

In the five years he had been doing this job, Joey had become adept at arranging the answer sheets. In the upper right hand corner of the part two booklets was a place to record the Part 1, Part 2 and final scores for each student. This made it easy for Joey to check each student's total score—using a calculator—and shuffle them either up or down according to the final score. Ordinarily Joey did this with little thought. However, whether it was an extra cup of coffee or a donut with extra sugar, this morning his brain was working along with his hands and he noticed something unusual about the scores reported by KCS. The Part 1 scores on many of the tests were identical and, when he finished rearranging them, the final scores seemed grouped just above the cut-off passing grade, which on this exam was sixty-five.

His interest stimulated, Joey took out a blank sheet of paper and, using a number-two pencil, wrote down the scores by five's from zero to one hundred on the edge of the sheet. He then made tally marks that corresponded to the final scores on each answer sheet. Now Joey was not a mathematician. In fact, he had barely gotten through the one statistics course that was required for all elementary education undergraduates at C. W. Post. If Joey were asked to describe the difference between "mean, mode, and median", he probably would have simply responded that the only difference was in their spelling and any talk about "standard deviation" and his mind would have completely shut down. However, he did vaguely remember something about distribution, specifically something about a bell-shaped curve being a normal distribution of scores within a group. When Joey looked at the tally marks for the scores from KCS, he could plainly see that the school's curve was what statisticians would call, "marked skewed to the right". That is, of the one hundred-two scores reported from KCS, eighty-two were in the sixty-five to sixty-nine range. Furthermore, while seventeen of the remaining twenty were evenly scattered from seventy to one-hundred range (one actually being a one-hundred), the other three were well below fifty—scores of forty-two, thirty-five and twenty-two to be exact. Even to one who was statistically challenged, this screamed for further investigation.

Taking the answer sheets from those eighty-two scores and spreading them out on his desk, Joey noticed he had been correct; the Part 1 scores for seventy-eight of the students in that group were the same! On further examination, not only were the scores the same but, aside from the student's name at the top of the paper, the answers to the questions were exactly the same as well. Only because the scores on the Part 2 differed slightly was the final score a bit different but not enough to cause a failing mark. While Joey was not exactly sure, he swore, after closer inspection, that these Part 1 answer sheets where, in fact, photocopies. Good copies to be sure, but nevertheless, copies.

This revelation sent Joey's mind spinning. To stop it, he got up from his desk, wandered over to the pencil sharpener, sharpened the pencil he had used and put it in the breast suit pocket. After some deliberation as to what to do, he decided to take his tally sheet to the room housing the computer that stored the test archives. He felt he needed to make some comparisons to earlier years. Once at the keyboard, he type Kaaterskill Central School into the computer and called up the results of the school's Competency Exams for the preceding five years. It was easy to find KCS scores since, unlike most other schools, which gave the Competency Exams two times a year, KCS only gave theirs in June. This meant he only needed to compare five sets of scores. A cursory examination of the results showed the school's Mathematics, Science and Social Studies exams seemed to be normally distributed. However, Joey could not help but notice that the English exams fit the same pattern as the tally sheet he had in his hand. It would not be too hard for anyone, even someone a lot duller than Joey, to figure out that there had been tampering done to the results of all six of these tests.

Had Joey been an honest and conscientious employee he would have blown the whistle on the school by immediately taking his suspicions to the head of the Testing and Evaluation Division. The division head would then take the information on up the chain of command until someone would be authorized to send a letter to the Chief School Officer at Kaaterskill Central School inquiring as to what was going on. The CSO would launch an investigation and, upon discovering the culprit, place him or her on paid leave. Next, the CSO would contact the State Educational Department concerning what exactly appeared to have happened. This would prompt the state to launch its own inquiry, which, if it proved that the tampering had taken place could result in the firing of teacher or teachers involved and invalidating their license(s). The school may or may not have some penalty assessed if the State Educational Department felt the school board or administration were aware of the problem prior to its discovery or were accessories to it. The time frame for this inquiry could be as long as five years, especially if the New York State Teachers' Association or the United Teachers of New York State got involved in defending those accused.

Joey was not concerned about this. As soon as he became aware that tampering had taken place, the extortion gene, which, apparently ran in the family, kicked in. *Here*, he thought, *was a situation where there was a possibility of profit.*

Joey's next thought was just as simple: *How is this going to earn me either money, prestige or both?*

Under the first option, he figured maybe he could somehow let the person or persons responsible come up with a sum of money to buy his silence—forgetting for a moment that these were undoubtedly teachers whose salaries would not allow for paying a great deal of bribe money. The second alternative, which might serve Joey better, would be to confront the perpetrators, get a confession and earn the state's undying gratitude. This would surely mean not only a raise in salary but also a more prestigious job. One thing for sure was that, if he took this option, Joey was not going to do it anonymously.

Either way he felt his first step was to go to KCS and talk to someone. Stuffing the KCS answer sheets along with his tally sheet in his briefcase and telling the secretary at the front desk that he was taking the rest of the week off for personal reasons; he headed back to his apartment. The secretary thought nothing of Joey leaving since this was his standard operating procedure. She just assumed he must be finished sorting the tests for this period and was entitled, therefore, to time off until the next bunch arrived.

Once back at his apartment, Joey called 411 to get the telephone number of the Kaaterskill Central School. Using the pencil in the breast pocket of his suit he wrote the number on the pad beside the phone for reference. He returned the pencil to his pocket in case he would need it later. Dialing the school and telling the secretary he was from the State Education Department, he asked to be put through to the Chief School Officer.

The CSO answered the phone on the second ring.

"District office, Dr. Everett Shay speaking."

"Good afternoon, Dr. Shay. You don't know me but my name is Joey Scalani and I work for the State Education Department, Testing and Evaluation Division."

"Yes, it is nice to hear from someone in the State Department. What can I do for you Mr. Scalani?" Shay was used to kissing up to those in Albany, especially since he had aspirations of possibly being there one day.

"It isn't what you can do for me; it is what I can do for you."

"And that would be?"

"Dr. Shay, in checking the results of your school's June English-8 Competency Examination I noticed some discrepancies in the scores."

"Discrepancies? Are you sure?"

"Most definitely, sir. Someone on your staff has been substituting photocopied Part 1 answer sheets for those done by some of your students."

There was a pause at the Kaaterskill end of the line. "This is a very serious accusation. Are you sure you have proof?"

"Most definitely, I have the answer sheets and while the copies are extremely well done, I believe an expert would be able to tell they are photocopies fairly easily."

"I take it that you have not been to your boss on this."

"Not yet, I felt it was better if I let you explain yourself before I did that."

I'm sure!, thought Shay, who was beginning to smell a shakedown. "Could I see what you have?"

"No problem, if you will tell me where Kaaterskill Central is located, I can come to you." Joey figured the best way to get the money or confession would be to go directly to the source.

"We're located in Snyder's Corners about eighty miles south of Albany, if that's where you are now."

"It is. I can be there whenever it is convenient to meet with you. How about tonight?"

"Not a good time, I have a board of education meeting tonight and they tend to run late. How about tomorrow night, at my office in the school, say eightish?"

"I'll be there."

"Ok, the school is not that hard to find, you'll come in on Route 618, just go through town and we're on the far side of town as you come from the north, on the right side of the road as you go by. Do not go in the front door. It will be locked, but go around to the back, I'll be waiting and let you in."

"Though town on Route 618, right side, and around to the back", Joey repeated the directions.

"And don't forget the answer sheets. Mr. Scalani, I'm as appalled as you are by this and I hope we can get to the bottom of it."

"I hope so too."

"See you at eight tomorrow. Good-bye."

"Right, Good-bye." Joey hung up.

All night Joey tossed and turned as his thoughts alternated between the prospect of easy money and the thought of hero status with a new, more prestigious position. The next morning he rose late, called the office to extend his personal leave, put on the suit he wore the previous day and left the apartment. He called the local Avis and arranged to rent a compact car—like his uncle, he also never owned a car for the much the same reasons. Picking the car up at noon, he first stopped at the corner drug store to buy a New York State map, locating Snyder's Corners on it while drinking a cup of coffee and eating a donut at Dunkin Donuts. He set out with great expectations.

****

When Everett Shay hung up the phone, he was an unhappy man. When he hired his old army buddy to teach English eight years ago he had no idea the man was so completely incompetent. It only took him a year to find that out. In his first year at KCS, Milt Meyers taught high school English but his students and their parents were so upset about the lack of stimulation, the content of the course, and Meyers' teaching methods (or lack thereof), that they gave Everett no choice but to reassign him. Rather than admit a hiring mistake, his options were two: find a vacant position where Meyers would do no harm, or create some meaningless position within the school system especially for Milt where he would be out of the way. Fortunately for Everett this quandary resolved itself when the eighth grade English teacher retired. Everett simply assigned Milt to the eighth grade position. That seemed, at the time, to be a good place to hide Milt since no one was sure what was taught in junior high English. The main requirement was just to keep to keep students under control. Unfortunately, Everett did not reckon with the English-8 Competency Examination.

After the state released the results of Milt's first year's English-8 Competency Examination, Everett realized, too late, that he had made another mistake. The scores were exceedingly low, especially when compared to surrounding schools of the same size and, even in relation to the scores this same group had on their English-6 Competency Examination. Hoping it might be an aberration, Everett let it slide. The scores the next year were even worse. Unfortunately for Everett and KCS, this was Milt's third, tenure-granting, year.

Had the procedure used to enter and check scores in Albany not created a three-month time lag between when a test was given and when the results were known statewide, Milt may well have been released at the end of that third year. However, since the administration and school board had no probable cause and since Milt was at the end of his probationary period, there was no recourse but to grant him tenure during the June board of education meeting. When the results of the English-8 Competency Examination finally reached Everett's desk at the end of September, it was too late, and unless Milt did something like having sex with a fourteen-year old student or downloading child porn, he had a job for life.

Everett realized he had to do something. Not so much to save Meyer's job but so Everett did not look bad for having recommended him for the position in the first place and to prevent the State Education Department from coming down on the school district by initiating procedures which could lead to the school being rated as "failing" or worse. Putting their heads together, Milt and Everett came up with the idea of substituting each failing student's Part 1 answer sheet with one that had enough correct answers on it to raise the score to passing.

Since there was more leniency in scoring of the Part 2, Milt, who corrected all the exams, could simply adjust his grading on the second part to assure the student's mark was above sixty-five. Of course, it did mean that the student's name had to be written in on each of the substituted answer sheets. This did not prove to be a real problem since all the poorer students printed their names in block letters using their number-two pencils which made them easy for Milt to forge. Using this technique it might have been possible to raise all the students' scores to passing but Milt and Everett agreed this was not a good idea and might be suspicious. For that reason, a few students, mostly those who gave Milt the hardest time during the year, kept their poor scores. Aside from authorizing it, Everett's main contribution to the fraud was to requisition the best photocopying machine money could buy and keeping it in his office. He even went so far as to contact a fellow Gulf War officer who was now working with the CIA to be sure that the model of the machine he purchased was the same as the one The Agency used to copy and forge documents.

While it seemed that what Everett was doing might be done out of compassion for his service buddy, this was not the case. In truth as time went on Everett barely tolerated Milt, thinking of him less and less as a colleague and more as an employee. While Everett had started his educational career as an English teacher, he very soon realized that he was not a good teacher, did not like the hours or amount of work he was asked to do—correcting essays was hell—and he was not receiving a decent salary. Since money was more important to him than working with students and, by the time he came to this point he already had enough years in the field to be eligible for an early retirement, his only option for continuing in education was in school administration. So while still teaching, he took evening and summer classes for certification in administration and, as soon as this was earned, took a high school principal job. In fact, he even went so far as to submit all his graduate hours to the State University in Albany and, after some finagling and a brief dissertation, the institution awarded him a Doctorate of Education. This allowed him to preface his name with the title "Dr" which looked impressive on his résumé and justified his feeling of superiority over his former colleagues.

The longer Everett served as an administrator and the higher he rose in the position, the less he remembered about what it was like to be a teacher. Gradually, he forgot it altogether and assumed an adversary position concerning all of his teachers, where the teachers became "them" rather than "us" in terms of setting and meeting educational goals. Teachers always wanted things like higher wages, more benefits, smaller class sizes and new textbooks. All of these things raised taxes. Since it was the Chief School Officer's job to budget for these and explain tax increases to the public, the teachers made Everett's job that much tougher and he resented it.

And, it got worse. As CSO, Everett's position forced him to take part in the negotiation sessions between the KCS Board of Education and the KCS Teachers' Association as the leader of the board's team. While Everett thought of himself as a shrewd negotiator, the truth was the union's negotiator beat him nine times out of ten. He then had to go back and humiliate himself in front of the board to sell the package, something that only made his dislike of the teachers more acute. Everett did manage one huge success however, when, the previous year he managed to bargain the teachers' salaries in at two percent less than the board was actually willing to go. Then, when constructing the current budget he used this extra money and some that would have gone for elementary school supplies, to give himself a hefty twenty percent raise. It was only because Milt was necessary for Everett to survive in his position without looking like a complete ass and to use this raise to increase his retirement's pension, that Everett continued in this conspiracy with Milt at all. That Milt never suspected he was being used was due to the fact that Everett had mastered the technique of lying to everyone without revealing his true feelings. This served Everett well as an administrator.

In the five years that Milt and Everett had been using this technique, Kaaterskill's English-8 Competency Examination's scores had been steadily rising. This improvement not only took Shay and Meyers off the hook but Meyers was actually cited by the state as a master teacher and given a certificate signed by the governor and Commissioner of Education. The only drawback was that Milt, because of the stress caused by adjusting these scores and fear that he would be discovered, would have a yearly PTSD episode shortly after the scores were released. Only after his vacation at a veterans' hospital and no indication from the State Ed Department that there was a problem with the scores, would Milt fully recover.

Aside from the two-week recovery period, there was no other problem, until today.

Everett had his secretary send an interschool memo to Milt that directed him to see Everett immediately after school.

Chapter 7

At three-fifteen, that afternoon there was a knock on Everett Shay's office door. He answered it, to find Milt Meyers standing there in his normally disheveled suit and tie. At first glance, Everett thought, *I hope Milt hasn't started on his annual PTSD breakdown.* On closer inspection, however, it seemed that this was Milt's normal attire and that he still had his wits about him.

Asking Milt to come in and sit down, Everett went around his desk, sat on the front edge and related the phone call from Joseph Scalani. Milt met the news with surprising calm, maybe because had he always felt, eventually, they would be caught, or maybe the reality had not sunk in.

"Ok", he said when Everett was finished, "What do we do now?"

"Obviously, we can't let this pissant of a state department flakey cause problems. I want you here tomorrow night and the two of us can see what exactly he has. It might just be a lucky guess, but if it is incriminating, we'll have to go from there."

"What do you suppose he wants?" Milt still did not seem worried.

"I'm not sure, but with a name of Scalani, it is probably some sort of shake-down for money." Everett watched a lot of Soprano episodes too. "We'll have to see if we can negotiate some sort of compromise."

"And get those answer sheets back?"

"Right. Now since I'm not expecting him until eight tomorrow night, it would be a good idea if you got here at, say, seven-thirty. Come in the front door. You have your key, right?"

"The one for the front door that I use when I come in to photocopy stuff? Sure." Milt answered his own question.

****

At seven-thirty the next evening Milt let himself into the front door of the school. The interior was dark, the only light coming from the red "EXIT" signs. Since Milt was used to finding his way to Everett's office under the cover of darkness, he had little trouble negotiating the dark hallways. That was until he bumped smack dab into Mike Case who was standing in the darkened corridor near the gym door, one arm around Katie Lasher.

"What the...?" Milt did not expect to see anyone, much less Mike with Katie, in the building.

"Hi Milt, what in hell are you doin' here?" Mike seemed slightly embarrassed. Katie slid around behind him. Considering Mike's size and shape, Katie immediately disappeared with only the top of her head showing since she stood several inches taller than Mike.

"Forgot some stuff in my room. How 'bout you?" *Shit*, Milt was thinking, *now I'll have to go to my room rather than directly to Everett's office*

"Not much, just checkin' on my boys."

****

Mike Case's "boys" were his basketball team. When hired as the physical education teacher at KCS, Mike was dismayed to find that the agreement between the KCS board of education and the KCS Teachers' Association specified that all physical education teachers were required to coach at least one interscholastic sport during the school year, unless there were no openings for coaches. Unfortunately for Mike, his first year also marked the year that Myron Bracey, the much beloved basketball coach at Kaaterskill Central School, retired. Since no one was willing to come forward to replace Bracey, Mike had no other choice to fulfill the terms of his contract or go back to the bluestone pit. He had to take the coaching job.

This terrified Mike. His only interscholastic athletic experience in either high school or college had been on the wrestling team as a freshman and sophomore at KCS. After his second year, his weight had ballooned to such a degree that the only weight class in which he could possibly have been eligible to compete was "unlimited" and, even there, he often exceeded the two hundred-fifty-pound upper limit. After several futile attempts to get down to this weight he quit and spent the rest of his academic career strictly as a spectator. This meant he had absolutely no experience as either a basketball player or coach, something that made no difference to the board of education or teachers' association; a contract being a contract.

There was one benefit, however. Given his inexperience the school board agreed to send him for a week, all expenses paid, to a National Association of Basketball Coaches clinic in New Orleans. Since this clinic coincided with Marti Gras, Mike thoroughly enjoyed his trip to the Big Easy. Unfortunately for him, the notes that NABC's staff generously supplied to the coaches so they would not have to actually attend the sessions, were left on a bar stool in Atlanta's Hartsfield Airport when Mike had to run to catch his connecting flight home. Thus, in spite of the board spending all that money, Mike learned zilch from the trip and only came back with several dozen glass bead necklaces. (On the other hand, that same year, two high school mathematics teachers had to pay their own expenses to a National Council of Teachers of Mathematics conference in Syracuse. The NCTM meeting was for the introduction of the new national requirements for high school mathematics. The school board generously allowed the teachers to use their sick leave days to attend this conference as long as they paid their own expenses.)

Given this auspicious start, Mike's basketball coaching career might well have been a disaster except for Cindy and William Jameson. Cindy, who had a PhD in Chemistry from Princeton, was the head of the Science Department at SUNY Oneonta. Her husband, William, whose Doctorate in English Literature was from Penn State, taught Afro-American studies at Hartwick. The Jamesons, both of whom were African-Americans, decided they did not want there twin sons, James and John, to grow up in the city so they bought an eighteenth century farmhouse on the western edge of the Kaaterskill school district, moving in the same year their sons entered the ninth grade. The addition of the Jamesons to the district not only raised the number of African-Americans in the school to two, but, with James and John entering the freshman class, increased the average IQ of that class by ten points.

The boys were not only very intelligent but were highly skilled athletically, being, at age fourteen, both six-foot two inches and growing. William Jameson had recognized his sons' basketball ability when they were entering sixth grade and, over his wife's objection, had made sure that they attended progressively more rigorous basketball camps each summer. As a result, by the time they entered Kaaterskill Central School, both boys were accomplished players, who, as twins, were always on the same wavelength and could hit each other in stride with an amazing number of no-look passes. Their entry into KCS coincided with Mike Case's first year as basketball coach of the KCS Dutchmen.

****

The school had adopted for their mascot the name "Dutchmen" as an attempt to honor the original settlers of the area. Although these settlers spoke what was erroneously called "Dutch", they had actually come from the Palatine area of Germany by way of Holland and spoke what more correctly was Deutsche or High German. However, the using of "Germans" as a nickname had not been considered a worthy alternative. Unfortunately for the nickname, it had been adopted before Title IX and the growth of girls' sports so it created an identity problem when it came to identifying the school's distaff teams. The board of education had vetoed the suggestion of "Dutchwomen" as sounding too mature for the girls of KCS whereas "Dutch girls" was likewise disallowed as too immature. As no other alternative was offered, the school created an oxymoron by calling the girls' teams the "Lady Dutchmen" which satisfied no one but had to suffice until some of the hidebound alumni would agree to a new moniker.

****

While he was not a skilled coach—he was wise enough to buy, using school funds, a set of Better Basketball Videos to tutor himself— Mike did recognize talent. Over the protests of parents who felt he was taking playing time away from their sons and thus denying them opportunities for college scholarships, Mike immediately promoted James and John onto the varsity basketball team. The results were instant. In combination with any three white players who were willing to sacrifice themselves on defense, the Jameson twins tore up the Catskill Mountain League, the Dutchmen going undefeated in the league and in the Section III, Class C Championships for the first three years the Jamesons played. The only thing that prevented them, as well as Coach Case, from winning the State's Class C title were a series of bad breaks.

Their first year the team got as far as the state quarter finals when, with KCS up by one and five seconds left in the game, John Connor, the KCS center, pulled down a defensive rebound and, for no apparent reason, went back up for a lay-in. KCS lost by one. The next year was equally bizarre. KCS, being the higher seed in the state semifinal game, was to be the home team in the scorebook. However, when Mike submitted his roster, he inadvertently used the team's away uniform numbers that were odd-numbered instead of the home, even-numbered uniforms the players were wearing that night. The mistake, discovered right at the opening tap for the game, caused KCS to be assessed five technical fouls for using players with the wrong uniforms. The opposing team's best foul shooter sank all the shots to put KCS down by five before they even started. KCS lost by three.

If anything, last year's screw up was more bizarre. Up by one with three seconds to go and with KCS in possession of the ball in the State,

Class C, Final, Mike signaled for a timeout to tell his team not to do anything stupid. Unfortunately, the timeout was Mike's sixth of the game, one more than the legally allowed five. Again the opposing team sent its best foul shooter to the line where he nailed the resulting two technical foul shots to ice the game and, once again, KCS went home a loser in their final game of the season. For the three white starters on the team who were seniors, this meant ending their final season with a loss. For Mike and the Jameson twins, while frustrated, at least they would have one more shot at the title.

Thus there was a reason for Mike Case to be standing in a darkened hall on that Thursday night in October The New York State Public High School Athletic Association, Inc. or NYSPHSAA, Inc., which oversees all interscholastic athletic competition in the state, sets seasonal coaching limits for high school student-athletes. The rule prohibits coaching in boys' basketball until the season officially begins on the first Monday of November. Until that date, while the members of the team are allowed to play together in any number of AAU and pick-up games, their high school coach cannot give instruction or be present in the gym during these sessions. The penalty for this would be to render the players ineligible for some or all of the season. (While reprimanding the coach was possible, aside from the loss of his players, there was no stigma involved.)

The NYSPHSAA, Inc. rule was causing Mike some problems.

Inasmuch as all of his other starters had graduated, it was necessary for the first time in four years to blend in three newcomers with the Jameson twins. Mike, recognizing his total lack of coaching skill, was worried that he would not have enough time to do this if he waited until November. Therefore, he devised a way whereby the basketball players, all of whom he prohibited from going out for football or soccer, could practice together in the gym each night beginning when school started in September. Since it would have been a rule violation if Mike were actually "in" the gym giving instructions he devised a quasi-legal solution. Because she was as a good if not a better coach than Mike, he used Katie Lasher to deliver his instructions from the hall to the players in the gym. Mike, consulting his notes from whichever video he last watched, would tell Katie what plays or drills he wanted them to work on and Katie would relate his desires to the Jamesons, who would interpret them for the other players and run them. Then Katie would come back to Mike with a report as to how well it worked. It was awkward, but it worked and neatly got around the NYSPHSAA, Inc.'s rule.

****

When Milt stumbled on to Mike and Katie in the hall, he saw not a romantic encounter but rather Mike demonstrating to Katie how a defensive player was to fight through a pick. That is not to say that Mike was not taking the opportunity to try to cop a feel in the process.

Since Mike was not too sure how Milt would report what he just saw, being primarily afraid he would be turned him in to NYSPHSAA,Inc., he told Katie to tell the boys to shower and leave. As soon as she went into the gym, he went out the back door. That is when he met a man in a suit standing in the parking lot.

"Are you Dr. Everett Shay?" The man had a downstate accent.

"Nope, you must be lookin' for the big guy. I noticed the light is on in his office. If you wanna wait a minute I'll take ya to him if ya want."

"No thanks, I have a meeting with him but I'm early. I'll just wait."

"Suit yerself." Mike got into his white Bronco and drove away, thinking no more about his encounter.

****

By the time Milt took a detour to his room and then carefully made sure he wasn't seen on his way to Everett's office, Joey Scalani was already there. He was sitting on a chair in front of Everett's desk, his brief case opened and KCS's packet of answer sheets spread out on the desktop. Everett was looking concerned.

"This certainly looks serious." Everett was saying as Milt walked in. "By the way, this is Milt Meyers, our Eighth Grade English teacher. I wanted him here to see if there is anything he might add."

Joey rose, tuned around and eyed Milt. He did not offer his hand.

"Milt", Everett continued, "this is Joseph Scalani from the State Education Department. He's the one who found what he thinks is a problem with last June's Competency Exams."

"Dr. Shay, I don't think there is a problem with your exam, I know there is one and it isn't just last year's exam either. From what I can tell this has been going on for a while. Either you or Mr. Meyers or someone not in this room, has replaced the student's Part 1 answer sheets with photocopied ones." Joey was indignant that Shay doubted his integrity.

"Are you sure? Let me see." Milt walked to the desk and picked up a copy. The one he chose was the one with the score of one-hundred. "This looks ok to me. I corrected this one and it was a perfect paper. In fact, the essay was so good it made me cry."

"I'm not talkin' about that one. Take a look at this." Joey handed Milt one of the ones with a score of sixty-six.

"Don't see any problem with it." Milt said.

"Look closer. That Part 1 is a photocopy. It's a good one, but it's a copy, I'm sure of it. If you doubt it, compare it to this one." Joey handed a second sheet to Milt, this one with a score of sixty-seven.

"I'll be damned, both Bobby Sutton and Malcolm Bates had exactly the same answers on Part 1." Milt was reading the student's names off the top of the answer sheet. "While I can't remember where they sat during the test, I'm sure I watched them carefully enough to see that they didn't cheat."

"If they cheated, Mr. Meyers, then so did all of these." Joey held up the other seventy-eight tests that had identical Part 1 answers. "Not only that, but the names at the top seem to be all printed by the same person. While I'm no handwriting expert, I bet if one were to look at them, he would say the same thing."

"Now who would do a thing like that?" Milt was referring to the forged names.

"While I'm not one hundred percent sure, Mr. Meyers, I'd be interested to know who, besides yourself, had access to these test results. I only see your name signed on the affidavit attesting that you and you alone corrected them."

"So you're saying I was the one that did this?" Milt's voice was rising as he tried his best to simulate anger.

"Now wait a minute." Always the facilitator, Everett broke in. "Nobody's accusing anyone of anything at this point."

"I am.", Joey reached over to pick up the papers. "Maybe not Mr. Meyers exactly, but from what I see here, there aren't too many possibilities. Unless you, Dr. Shay, are also involved."

"OK, let's see what we have." Everett was ready to be conciliatory before things got out of hand and Scalani left in a huff. If he turned what he had over to someone higher up, it could cause them real problems. That would put him and Milt in deep doo-doo. Having served on a number of negotiation sessions with the KCS Teachers' Association, he thought he knew how to handle a situation like this. "I'm sure that neither Mr. Meyers nor I have anything to do with this problem. But, let's assume there is someone on my staff that did this. What do we have to do to make the problem go away? I want to keep my district out of this kind of thing."

Now it was Joey's turn to make a decision. Would he go for the money or blow the whistle? On the drive down, he had batted both possibilities around in his head. It was a toss-up. This time the coin landed "heads".

"I'm thinking of ten thousand dollars." Joey had decided, in one of the conversations with himself, that that was a nice number and probably doable for anyone on a teacher's salary.

"No way!" Milt looked like he'd been doused with cold water.

Ah ha, I was right, Everett though, *it is a shakedown.* "That's a lot of money. I couldn't come up with that amount out of the district's petty cash and, even if I could, I certainly don't have it here."

"Ok, I'll make it easy on you. Five thousand now and five thousand next month. In addition, I want a written confession from both of you that I will hold and return once the money is fully paid." Might as well try for hero status too, Joey thought.

"You're crazy. Like Everett said, there is still no way we could come up with that much money, and I won't confess to something I never did!" Milt was still trying to weasel out.

Everett was taking another tack, however. "Ok, on second thought, at that amount, maybe we can make a deal. But I obviously don't have that kind of money here now. I'll need time to raise it."

"OK, how much time?"

"At least until tomorrow night. I'll tell you what, come to my house tomorrow night, again at eight o'clock, and I'll have the five thousand for you."

"But no confession! And we want those answer sheets too" Milt added, still wondering where in hell Everett was going to come up with five grand in twenty-four hours.

"Yes a confession. But I'm a reasonable man. Give me the five thousand and the confessions and I'll return both confessions and the answer sheets when I get the rest of the money. Of course if, after a reasonable amount of time, I don't get the rest of the money, I turn you both over to my boss and tell him you tried to bribe me to keep me quiet as well."

That would be the best of both worlds, thought Joey.

"Sounds ok with me. Milt, do you agree?" Everett gave Milt a look he could not quite interpret.

"I guess, if that's what you wanna to do, but I still don't like the idea of a confession being out there."

"Fine, then we're in agreement." Everett gave one of his best fake conciliatory smiles—the kind he had developed for board members, contract negotiators, parents and State Ed Department supervisors. He sounded satisfied, like he's just finished up another three-year contract. "Here are directions to my house. It is easy to find. It's just a couple of miles further down Route 618 past the school. It's a doublewide that sits back from the road a ways—name's on the mailbox. We'll see you there at eight tomorrow." He handed Joey the map he had drawn on a piece of his stationery that had the heading removed so it could not be traced.

Joey studied the map. Orienting it in such a way that he understood it and, having no questions, he folded it and put it in his pocket. "Eight o'clock." He repeated the time as he gathered up the answer sheets from the desk, took the two out of Milt's hand, and put them in his brief case. Closing the briefcase he said, "I better be going."

"Good idea. Be careful you aren't seen. Milt and I will stay a few minutes. It is better if we aren't seen together."

"Right, I'll find my way out." Joey left the room, closing the door behind him.

Waiting until he was sure Scalani was gone, Walt turned to Everett and asked, "How in hell are we gonna come up with that kinda money?"

Everett looked at his old army buddy, gave that smile again and said. "We're not."

****

Everett Shay had developed a knack for standing aside from his life and examining it without regard to morality. This ability helped him as an administrator and also kept him sane when he had to perform some nasty task with messy results. As a result, while Everett's experience in the Gulf War went far beyond those that gave Milt Meyers nightmares, he felt no qualms about what had happened.

Just two weeks before his assignment to the motor pool where he met Milt Meyers, Everett was on a combat mission during which his squad captured two Iraqi militiamen. As superior officer on the mission and being tired of tramping around in the sand, Everett assigned himself to escort these captives back to camp and turned the patrol over to his sergeant. On the way back to the detention center, a sandstorm came up and the three of them, none of whom had ever been in the desert before, became hopelessly lost. After spending the night huddled out of the wind and running low on water, Everett realized he could not get to safety with the burden of the captives so he simply tied them together and left them. A day later, after Everett had been rescued, he tried to lead a patrol back to where he left the men but since his trail had been covered by drifting sand and, without any landmarks, this proved futile. The captives were never located and the Army simply forgot about Everett's moment of indiscretion.

The fact that Everett left two men to die in the desert never bothered him. He simply rationalized that they were the enemy, it was he or they, and let it go at that. Now, it would seem he was about to embark on another chapter in his life that would require the same kind of compartmentalization.

Chapter 8

It was getting dark when Milt pulled into Everett's driveway. He could see Everett in his garage working on his 2004 Polaris Sportsman 400. Leaving the car, he walked over.

"Got a big ATV run tomorrow. Have to get 'er tuned up for it." Everett looked up from where he had just finished tightening in a new spark plug.

Everett was big on ATV runs. Using the skills he had acquired during his time in the motor pool in the Army, he would modify his machines from their factory settings so they had more power and ran faster. Everett loved the anonymity of these runs, where he could don a Darth Nader-like helmet/mask and blow away twelve-year olds as well as adults with his souped-up machines.

He had purchased the Sportsman new two years ago and had spent a lot of time and money modifying it. It was the four-stroke, 425cc model with liquid cooling engine and painted the original "sportsman" green. Everett had wanted a camouflaged model since it was less likely to show wear but, unfortunately, by the time Everett bought this one, Big Ed was out of that particular paint job. The green was Everett's second choice. This model of ATV was intended for use by outdoorsmen in hunting thus it came fitted with the necessary racks for carrying cargo and carcasses as well as a custom holster to hold a shotgun or rifle ready at hand. While Everett had every intention of using it in the woods, he also wanted it for ATV racing so he had taken it to a machine shop in Oneonta and had it rebored for oversized pistons. Once home, Everett added new exhaust pipes, tweaked the carburetor by putting in some new, special-order jets and added an after-market clutch kit. Now instead of a factory authorized top speed in the twenty-five to thirty miles per hour range, it could, under the right conditions, easily hit seventy. The "bike" had originally set Everett back six grand but now, with his modifications, it was worth well over a couple thousand more. He was proud of his work and it showed by the loving care he took of the machine.

"Big-time run over at Hensenville tomorrow afternoon. Gotta have this baby in top shape." He hopped on the machine, started it and with an ear shattering roar made a wide circle in the yard before pulling it up onto the trailer which was hitched to back of his pickup truck.

Milt could not help but admire the skill with which Everett handled the machine. He knew ATV's could be tricky.

"I take it our boy's not here yet." Milt said once the roar of the ATV had died down and the ringing in his ears had stopped.

"It's early. Why don't you come in the house to wait?"

Everett's house was actually a doublewide that he bought secondhand from the brother of the school board president for a fraction of the asking price. He especially liked the location. It was so far out of town that students, parents, teachers or the board members did not bother him yet it was close to some prime deer cover. It fit his needs, as being cheap and not exactly permanent. He had never had any intention of staying in Snyder's Corners anyway; he just hoped to remain in the community until he reached retirement age. He had simply taken the KCS's Chief School Officers job because it was a monetary step up from his last position as a high school principal and the extra pay meant he would get a boost in his final three years' salary. Since his retirement income was a percentage of that last three years income, this job meant a healthy increase in his pension. Unless an offer from the State Education Department came along, he figured he would retire from Kaaterskill Central in two more years and move to New Mexico where, he understood, they had year-round ATV runs.

The floor plan of the doublewide, in order to create the impression of a larger home, combined the living room and kitchen into one large open space. Between the two rooms was a divider/counter that served as an eating area as well as providing a flat surface on which to unload mail, car keys, bric-a-brac or whatever. Everett had several stools placed around the divider where guests were able to sit and lean on the counter. Everett was not, as far as he knew or cared, married, so the necessity of keeping the place picked up was not a priority. He had been married once, a long time ago, but his wife was not willing to subordinate her life to his and moved out—the fact that she found him *in flagrante delicto* with an ex-student, undoubtedly hastened her departure.

****

The incident occurred when his wife walked into Everett's office and found the girl on her knees under his desk—Everett being seated, at the time, at the desk sans trousers. Fortunately for Everett, the girl was nineteen and had graduated the year before so he was not in any legal trouble. Also neither his wife nor the girl felt the need to report the incident so the affair never became public. This was equally fortunate since it had been ongoing for a year prior to the girl's high school graduation when the she had worked as an intern in his office. This could have been put him in a bit of a legal bind, had it come out. His wife was fairly understanding about the whole thing and they agreed that, since the act was fellatio it was not, after all, real sex and should be an overlooked discretion. (It should be noted that, at the time, both Shays were registered Democrats who later switched party allegiance due to Clinton's indiscretion.) Two months later, citing incompatibility and a need to live her own life, his wife left him. He had not heard from her since so did not know, nor did he care, if she had ever filed for divorce.

Everett and the girl continued their liaison until Everett went to Iraq, at which point she found someone closer to her own age and sent Everett a "Dear John" letter. This was actually a relief to Everett since he no longer had the stamina to keep up with the younger woman anyway. He had been, in fact, looking for a way to break it off without pissing her off in such a way that she would report him and jeopardize his educational career. It was, however, his last relationship with the opposite sex; with the exception of the hookers he employed while attending various administration conferences around the country. The school board, unbeknownst to them, paid for these liaisons through Everett's expense account.

His only passion now was his ATV.

****

Milt took one of the stools, pushed aside a partially filled cup of coffee and sat. Putting one elbow on the counter he leaned forward and asked.. "Well, what are we gonna do?"

Everett did not sit but, rather, paced in the kitchen area. "I've done some thinking. First, obviously, we can't and aren't going to give this dickwad a penny. Second, we can't let him take what he has to his boss. The results would be a disaster for both you and the school system. I've run some preliminary budget figures for next year and, unless the legislators raise state aid, we're going to have to raise the tax rate eight percent. We can't afford the loss of even one student and I know for sure if they go so far as to take over the district parents like the Jamesons would pull their kids out."

"That would be tough on our basketball team." Milt offered.

"Not to mention what would happen if the budget was defeated. Basketball, as well as all the rest of the sports, would go down the tubes."

"So you've got a plan?" Milt moved the half-empty coffee cup to the far side of the counter so he would not spill it.

"I said I've been thinking about it. How about if we try to scare our little buddy into thinkin' we'll cause him bodily harm? Maybe that way we can get the answer sheets away from him and destroy them. Without the sheets, basically, he's got nothin'. We'll be in the clear. After all, it's our word against his. As two upstanding educators, hell, you've even got a teaching award for Christ sakes, and we're war vets to boot. He wouldn't stand a chance."

Milt, inadvertently rubbing his chin, nodded his head in agreement. "Might just work." His mood lightened a bit at the thought.

It was dark when they heard the sounds of a car in the driveway. Everett went to a switch panel next to the front door and turned on the yard light. With the area bathed in light, Milt, looked out the front window in time to see a rental car pull slowly up to the house and stop. After a short period of time Joey Scalani emerged, still wearing the same suit he had on the previous two days. He looked around to get his bearings.

Hell, Milt thought, *doesn't he own any other clothes?*

****

In truth, Joey was still wearing his only suit because he did not go back to Albany the previous night. Too excited to drive, he had taken a room at the Holiday Inn in Oneonta. There he managed a fitful night's sleep followed by a decent breakfast. Needing something to kill time, he then spent most of the morning at the Soccer Hall of Fame, reading the plaques of the inductees and looking at the exhibits. That afternoon Hartwick and his alma mater, C.W. Post, were playing a soccer match on the adjoining field and Joey found himself a bit excited rooting for his alma mater. Post lost the exhilarating match 1 – 0. After a leisurely supper, he drove to Snyder's Corners feeling fairly satisfied with himself since he was on the cusp of pulling off, what appeared to be, a huge financial coup.

****

Joey's step was light as he went up the porch steps to the doublewide, briefcase in hand, and rang the bell. Everett Shay opened the door.

"Well, I see you found it." Everett offered his normal, publicity smile.

"Using your map, it wasn't hard." Joey did not smile back but look around inside. "Nice place you have here." He then noticed Milt sitting at the divider and nodded.

"Good evenin'." Milt said, not putting much of any emotion into the greeting.

"Well, let's get right down to business, shall we? I'm sure you'll want to be getting back to Albany." Everett motioned to the stool across from Milt so Joey would be sitting with his back to the kitchen area.

Joey took the seat, moving it noticeably further from Milt, placed his briefcase on the counter and loosened the buttons on his suit coat. "Do you have the money and the confessions for me?"

"Yes and no. There has been a bit of change in plans. How would you feel about havin' the whole amount now?" Everett was in the kitchen facing both men. Joey had to turn to look at him. Milt, as usual, did not have any idea where Everett was going with this, so he just sat back and kept his mouth shut.

"Change in plans?" Joey was puzzled but not so much as to stop and think how, if Shay and Meyers balked at five grand last night, they could have come up with ten today. If he had been a seasoned conman, he might have smelled a rat.

"Yes, after Mr. Meyers and I thought it over, we decided it wouldn't be prudent to have a confession floating around, the answer sheets would be incriminating enough. So, by doing a bit of digging for funds, we managed to come up with the full ten thousand."

Joey was delighted beyond belief.

"If I remember correctly, you agreed to turn over the answer sheets to us upon full payment. In addition, since we are paying in full, there should be no need for confessions. Am I right?"

"That is correct." Joey opened his brief case and removed the packet of answer sheets, laying them on the counter. For full effect, he decided to fan them out. This looked so good he could not help but sit back and admire his work.

This was a mistake since it gave Everett the opening he needed.

Everett's initial plan had been, as he told Milt, to scare hell out of Joey to convince him to turn over the answer sheets and forget about the whole thing. To make this plan effective, it meant that he would have to rough Joey up a bit to show him they meant business. Seeing that Joey was concentrating on the brief case and the answer sheets, Everett felt this was his chance to strike the first blow.

Once, when Everett was first married and starting his job as high school principal, his wife, as a joke, gave him a large wooden paddle to hang in his office. The paddle, carved out of red oak it had the words "Board of Education" wood-burned into its flat end. As long as he was a high school principal he kept it on display on the wall of his high school office but when he became a Chief School Officer he felt since he dealt directly with an actual school board of education, it was not appropriate thing to display. Not willing to hide it completely, he hung it above his cupboards in his kitchen. When he noticed that Joey was preoccupied with the papers, Everett reached up, grabbed the paddle by the handle and, aiming at the back of Joey's head, he swung—hard.

The paddle made contact with the back of Joey Scalani's head, sounding like a pumpkin being hit by a baseball bat. He made a small sigh and fell forward. The stool went out from under him as he toppled over, face down, onto the counter. His head, bleeding quite profusely where the edge of the paddle lacerated his scalp, came to rest in the briefcase.

Milt, who was shocked by the suddenness of the attack, leapt off his stool and let out an "Oh My God, what did you do?"

"That'll teach that little pissant to mess with me. Now, when he comes to, maybe he'll see how serious we are and we can talk some sense into him. You keep an eye on him to make sure he doesn't wake up while I go get something to tie him up." Everett replaced the paddle on the wall and started to go out the door.

"Wait a minute." Milt was leaning over Joey. "I don't think he's breathin'."

"What?" Returning, Everett reached down and took one of Joey's wrists. He did not feel a pulse. "I didn't hit him that hard."

"Well, you musta hit him in the right place, then, 'cause he's a goner." Milt had had enough first aid in the service to know what kind of response an unconscious man would have.

What neither Milt nor Everett knew was that the blow to the back of Joey's head had forced him off the stool and caused his loosened suit coat to swing open. This allowed the number-two pencil he had been carrying in his breast pocket to swing out and become perpendicular to his chest. At the same time, Joey's body had to obey Newton's first Law of Motion. This meant that the forward momentum generated by the combination of the blow to the head, the fall, and coupled with his weight, forced his body onto the pencil in such a way that when his upper torso hit the divider/counter, the pencil penetrated his chest, missing his ribs, and neatly severed the aorta. Deprived of blood, his heart gave a few final pumps and stopped. Death followed immediately.

Unaware of this—the hole was so small and the pencil plugged it so effectively that there was no exterior blood at the site of the wound— Milt and Everett could only conclude that the blow to the head had killed Joey. Later, when they moved the body, the coat to fell back over the chest so the end of the pencil, which protruded slightly, did not show. Fortunately, since Joey's head had landed in the briefcase, what little blood had come off his scalp was contained there and did not reach the counter. In fact, except for the toppled stool and the liquid on the counter was from the spilled coffee, it was a fairly clean crime scene.

"Now what are we gonna do?" asked Milt.

"Give me a chance to think." Everett was looking around as if he hoped there would be clues to a solution some place in his house. He was, after all, not used to having a dead body lying on his kitchen counter; much less one for which he was responsible. Once he gathered his wits, Everett moved out the door and into his front yard looking for some—any—solution to his dilemma.

His first stop was at the car that Joey had driven. Joey had left the keys in the ignition. Everett opened the glove compartment and found the car rental agreement including a completed, signed credit card receipt.

The idiot had even opted for additional insurance. Everett thought.

Everett did realize this would make it easy for them to return the car, all they had to do was drop it off at the Avis lot in Albany. The thought occurred to Everett that, just maybe, he would place the body in the trunk, drop off the car and let the employees find it when the cleaned the trunk. Then it occurred to him that there would be questions as to how the car got to the lot since, obviously, Joey could not have driven it there himself.

There has to be some better way to get rid of that body. Everett thought.

That is when his eyes went to the ATV.

Going into the garage, he emerged with the racks for the front and back of the vehicle and a large, blue, plastic tarp. The racks, used to carry cargo, slid neatly into fittings on the front and back of the ATV.

He carried the tarp into the house.

"Here, help me roll him up in this." Everett spread the tarp out on the kitchen floor.

With some difficulty, Milt and Everett were able to roll the body onto the tarp and wrap it up; tucking both ends in like one would if they were making a giant burrito. With Milt on one end and Everett on the other, they carried the package out to the yard where Everett motioned with his head to the front rack on the Sportsman. They laid the body on the rack, much like one would have done with a deer carcass—this being the most common use of this kind of accessory—and Everett went into the garage for some bungee cords to secure it.

"We'll take the body out someplace and dump it." Everett talked as if he was stating the obvious.

"What do you mean by 'We'?" Milt was already exhausted from the exertion of moving the body from the house to the ATV. "What am I supposed to do, run along side while you drive that thing? It's only designed for one person."

"Nonsense, that's why I put on the rear rack. You just get in there and ride along. I've beefed the power up enough on this thing so it'll carry all three of us easily." Everett started the machine, gunned the motor, pointed to the rear rack and motioned Milt to get on.

Reluctantly, Milt climbed on, and tried to make himself comfortable by sitting on the rack with his legs and feet dangling off the back. "Where to?" he inquired over the engine noise.

"We'll just take some back trails through the woods to where Route 618 meets the trail into Loomis Pond—I know a lot of trails that we used to take when I was doing ATV tours. We'll only be on 618 a short way so no one will see us. We can dump him out by the pond."

Once at the clearing near the pond, they used the headlight on the ATV to locate the biggest mass of brambles they could find. After taking the body out of the tarp, Everett went though the trouser and jacket pockets, removing the piece of paper with the school phone number on it, some change and Joey's wallet—he wanted to make it as hard to identify the body as possible. Then with Milt grabbing the arms and Everett the feet, they tossed the body of Joseph Anthony Scalani as far as they could into the blackberry patch. While Everett checked to make sure he had hidden the body well and began refolding the tarp, Milt hopped on the ATV to turn it around. Being unpracticed in ATV operation—the Sportsman had a turning radius of slightly less than seven feet—he misjudged on how much room he needed and how quickly the machine started. As a result, he smacked into a mass of sumac trees at the edge of the trail at a fairly high rate of speed.

"Damn it, be careful!" Everett cried from where he was putting the finishing touches on the tarp. "You can chip the paint off that thing you know."

Returning to Everett's house, he noticed that Milt was not looking so good. "This would be a good time for your 'military leave."

"I think so."

"Ok, I'll tell you what you're gonna do. Go home and pack your stuff, then call me. I'll bring you back here and you can drive the rental car to Avis in Albany. The paper work is all done and in the glove compartment so all you have to do is drop it off. Everything's signed so you don't even have to even go in. Use this money", Everett took all the folding money out of Joey's wallet and handed it to Milt. "to take a bus to the VA hospital in Canandaigua and check yourself in. When you're ready to come home, call me and I'll come get you."

Milt thought it sounded like a good plan. Though shaken, he managed to get into his car and drive home to pack. Everett went into his house to straighten up the mess.

****

One of the things Everett learned early in his career as an administrator was to appear to be interested in his staff's problems. The trick he used to confirm the ploy was to write reminder notes to himself. Whenever a member of his staff had some kind of problem and brought it to Everett's attention, the first thing Everett did was find a piece of paper, write down the problem and carefully tuck the note in his shirt pocket. Done in the presence of the employee and with the proper amount of concern, this gave the appearance that Everett was interested in finding a solution to the problem. However, unless the solution was self-serving, Everett usually just forgot about the note and the piece of paper would turn up as a mass of paper-pulp in the pocket of a freshly laundered shirt. The note writing had become a habit, however, one that he was to apply right now.

As soon as Milt left and he got the house back into what would passed for normal, Everett took the contents of the briefcase and placed them in a large brown envelope. Using the paper cutter he had "borrowed" from the school he chopped off the letterhead from a piece of school stationery, and with the pen he kept handy for doing his grocery list, wrote "DISTROY THESE" on the scrap as a reminder to himself. Then, rather than following his usually habit of putting the note in his pocket, he paper clipped it to the outside of the envelope. His plan was to take the envelope to school and run its contents through the office shredder; he just wanted to be sure he did not forget. When Milt returned, Everett would give him the briefcase and the wallet to dispose of along the highway some place on route to returning the car.

Later, when Everett was reloading the ATV onto the trailer, he noticed a big scratch on front fender. He was not pleased.

Chapter 9

Phyllis Nielsen and Jimmy Kalid spent most of their first weekend in bed, rising only when Phyllis went into the kitchen to make them some peanut butter sandwiches—they found they both shared a postcoital craving for peanut butter sandwiches. Sunday afternoon they were eating this snack on the sofa, she was just in her bathrobe, he in his boxers. The cat was curled up between them, asleep. With the strains of Norah Jones' *Come Away With Me* CD coming from her stereo, Phyllis filled Jimmy in on her life; from an idyllic childhood in southern Minnesota up to, and including, her affair with the elementary principal.

Finished, she asked "How about you?"

Jimmy had not thought about his past in a long time. Nevertheless, he felt a comfort with Phyllis he had never felt with any woman before, so once he started, his whole life story just came tumbling out.

****

Jimmy's father had been born in Lebanon and emigrated to the United States as a teenager, fleeing the 1976 civil war. He found his way into upstate New York where he met his wife to-be, a first generation American of Lebanese decent, while he was working as a mechanic at her father's trucking company. Jimmy, their first born, came along just at the time his father struck out on his own, opening a small trucking company in Buffalo, New York. Jimmy remembered his childhood as an easy one in which he, his two brothers and three sisters seemed to have everything they needed in the way of home, food and love.

Jimmy was a better than average student in school and a decent athlete, his specialty being lacrosse. While not particularly big for his age, he was agile. Since he had developed powerful arms from helping his dad load and unload trucks on the weekends and over the summers, he combined his agility with this strength into a quick and powerful shot. Had the universities on the East coast that played the game scouted him and offered him one of the few scholarships given at the time, he would have jumped at it. It was just his luck, however, that Buffalo was not a hotbed of lacrosse and his high school never got as far as the state championships. Therefore, Jimmy went undiscovered.

Upon graduating from high school, he was accepted at Buffalo University, and by using a couple of minor academic scholarships, taking out a student loan, working part time for his father, and living at home, he managed to come up with enough money to make it through his four years and earn a BA in English. Upon graduation, he found that an English degree qualified him for next to nothing in the way of employment so, doing what ninety-nine percent of all English majors did, he took out another loan and entered grad school. In his case, he enrolled in NYU to work toward a master's degree in Elizabethan Literature. Although he had completed the required course work by August of 2001, he was running low on funds and, putting his thesis on the back burner, decided to find employment right after Labor Day.

Given the events that occurred in NYC that September, this turned out to be a lousy time for someone whose surname was Kalid and who had a swarthy complexion, to find work. Despite the fact that he, as well as the rest of his family, were Christians—Catholics to be precise, although Jimmy had not been in a church since high school— prospective employers were reluctant to hire him. The best he could do for the next two years were a series of menial jobs, mostly dealing with fast food services while he completed the thesis. Even this degree, however, was not making him any more employable. Maybe, given the area and the amount of education, the extra degree was actually making things worse.

Discouraged, he sought counsel from his graduate advisor who, having seen Jimmy help his fellow students, suggested he might make a good teacher. Also, the advisor told him that if he were to teach in an area that was considered Appalachia, he could very well have a large portion of his student loans forgiven. With this in mind, Jimmy went to the State data bank of teaching openings and found one for a high school English teacher posted from Kaaterskill Central School, which, as luck would have it, was economically and politically, if not geologically, considered part of Appalachia. Jimmy applied in September of 2004, and since the school year had started and the principal was desperate; he was hired, sight unseen, based solely on his resume. As it turned out, his English degree, since he had taken a smattering of education courses, was good enough for Jimmy to gain employment as a teacher. In addition, because he had the master's degree, it also meant he could forgo any further requirements for a permanent license. Now free of much of his financial obligation and education requirement he was able to enjoy teaching.

That is how he ended up in Snyder's Corners and in Phyllis Nielsen's bed.

Finishing his story, Phyllis kissed him and then, teasingly, asked. "How about your love life? You didn't mention anything about that. I told you about mine, now you have to tell me about yours."

To tell the truth, Jimmy did not have that much of a romantic past. Sure a few encounters during high school and college, some briefly sexual in nature. His longest romance was with a Fine Art's major during the year he was at NYU. They had moved in together early that summer—she moving into his one room apartment. When he awoke on the morning of September twelfth, all of her stuff was gone and all she left was a note on the table that simply said "Good Bye". Other than the Oneonta psych major, which he did not see any reason Phyllis need know about, there was no one else until Phyllis came along.

****

"That's all of it." Jimmy was finished. "Now you know everything there is about me."

"And I like it." Their sandwiches gone, she snuggled closer

With the Jones' CD on the second play through and Norah singing "*Turn me On*", Phyllis slipped her arms around him, the robe came off and the cat scurried for the bedroom. Later, someone was going to have to go to the Tavern for Jimmy's Jeep and the Stop 'N Go for more peanut butter and bread. The AP English essays were all going to get very good grades.

****

Using the return address from Joey's most recent thank you note, Tony Torrelli had no problem locating his late nephew's apartment. He remembered that part of town from his years of working in Albany as being an area of saloons and whorehouses. Now landlords, with HUD grants, had come in, bought out all the owners for pennies on the dollar, razed the buildings and put up apartment complexes, condos, and town houses. Not aware what the currently going rate was for bribes, Tony offered the super of the building a fifty to let him into Joey's apartment. The super, one of those displaced by the conversions done to his old neighborhood, gladly accepted and let Tony in.

The place looked exactly like what Tony would have expected, knowing his nephew. The walls were devoid of pictures, there were no books, newspapers or magazines in evidence anywhere. Looking in the refrigerator, all he found there was a carton of milk, a partly filled egg carton, some moldy cheese, and several half eaten containers of Chinese take-out. There was a stack of pizza boxes on top of the stove. As Tony walked by the desk, he noticed a pad beside the telephone. Finding a pencil in the desk drawer, Tony darkened the top page of the pad to bring out two phone numbers that had been written on the last page before it had been torn off the pad.

He called the second number, since it was local, first.

"Avis Rental, Ronald speaking, how may I help you?"

Thinking quickly Tony answered. "This is Joseph Scalani, I rented a car from you last week and now I can't find a package I purchased on my trip. Did I perhaps leave it in the rental?"

"How do you spell your last name?" Ronald asked.

"S as in Sam, C as in cat, A as in apple. L as in legal, A in apple again, N as in nothing and I as in Italy."

"Ok. Just hang on a second and I'll have one of the boys in the shop check." Music, which Tony did not recognize, filled his ear.

After what seemed to Tony to be thirty minutes but was more like five, Ronald came on again. "Mr. Scalani? I'm sorry, that car was rented out again on Monday. Tommy, the boy I talked to, remembers checking it when it was dropped off on Friday night but doesn't remember any package. We're understaffed today since it is Sunday, but if you'll call back on Monday there may be someone in then that would remember having seen it. How big a package are we talking about?"

"It was quite large so if your man didn't see it, then I probably left it elsewhere. Forget about it. It isn't that important. I'll look around here again. Maybe it'll turn up. Thanks for your time." Tony hung up and began to sort things out in his head.

So, he thought, *Joey probably rented that car to go to that damn hick town where he died. Since Isabel told us that the coroner said Joey died on either Friday or Saturday, it must have been Friday. Then whoever killed him must have brought the car back that night.*

With this making sense to him, Tony dialed the first number on the pad. It rang six times before an answering machine picked up.

"Kaaterskill Central School. Our switchboard is closed now, so either call us back on Monday morning or you may leave a message after the beep."

111

Without waiting for the beep, Tony hung up. Kaaterskill Central School, where in hell is that, Tony thought. On a hunch, Tony took out his cell phone and punched up a number on his speed dial.

"Dis is Charley, wadda ya want." The voice on the other end had a heavy New York City accent.

"Charley, dis is Two Toes, a coupla years ago you worked a scam selling school supplies." Tony easily slipped into the accent without missing a beat.

"Yeah, wadda 'bout it?"

"Ever hear of a Kaaterskill Central School?"

"Yeah, in some jerkwater town upstate. The asshole running it is a putz. Why?"

"Where is it located?"

"I dunno, like I said some two bit town, didn't even have a decent Italian restaurant. Christ, I worked alota places, can't remember 'em all"

"It wasn't Snyder's Corners, by any chance?" Tony figured it was worth a try.

"Yeah, that's it! Snyder's Corners, wadda crap hole."

"Thanks Charley, I owe ya."

"Yeah, but you'll never pay." Charley was not kidding.

Both lines went dead at the same time.

Bingo, Tony thought. Sticking the pad in his pocket, Tony locked his nephew's apartment door and went to his car. Stopping at the corner drug store for a New York State map, he located Snyder's Corners and took off.

The clerk at the drug store thought; *Strange, that's the second New York State map I've sold in the past week and it isn't even tourist season.*

****

The events of the previous night never bothered Everett and he had a good time at the following day's ATV run. However, the scratched paint on the Sportsman had been bothering him. It was not that he was concerned about the paint left when they dumped the body—he wasn't even aware that it was possible for a crime lab to match paint with a vehicle's model and year—it was simply because the ATV didn't look good. Half of being in these ATV runs was winning; the other half was in looking good doing it. Although the scratch was not that big and hardly noticeable, he did not think he looked good with a scratched vehicle, and was determined to have it repainted.

Therefore, when he got home from school on the following Monday afternoon he loaded the ATV on the trailer and hauled it over to Bob's Collision Repair Shop in Oneonta ("We Specialize in Deer Collision Repair."). For a reasonable amount, Bob was more than happy to repaint the vehicle completely. He even promised to mask it so that not a drop of paint would end up where it was not supposed to be. Inasmuch as the deer-rutting season was just beginning—his busiest time of year for repair and repainting—he said he would get right at it and promised Everett he could pick up the repainted ATV in a week. Everett chose candy apple red for the new color. Now that would look really good!

This left him at loose ends the following weekend with no ATV to tinker with, so he spent part of Sunday wandering through the woods behind his property looking for deer signs. He had buried a block of salt in the woods, to create a salt lick to attract deer—something that was highly illegal but only if the DEC caught him doing it. He found a rub that indicated a large buck was frequenting the area, probably searching for receptive does.

****

Moe had had a good Thursday, Friday and Saturday. He managed to track down all thirty of the ATV's at the top of his list. Since they were all less than two years old, it was not too hard to tell if they had lost paint. Of the first thirty, only five had been damaged. This included a machine that been totaled when its owner lost control and hit a tree three weeks before. Considering that the owner was in the hospital in traction, he certainly was in no position to have moved a body. The other damaged ones belonged to ATV run drivers all of whom had airtight alibis. They all could produce witnesses who had either seen them scrape paint in rollovers had on course collisions or could verify their whereabouts for every day of the previous weekend. Therefore, Moe was going into Monday with thirty down; twenty-one to go and the last ones were all close to Snyder's Corners. He figured that he should have his suspect tracked down no later than Tuesday.

****

On Monday morning, anyone seeing Phyllis would have realized there had been a change. She wore a blouse, skirt, her hair was down, and she wore eye shadow and lip-gloss. While Phyllis and Jimmy tried everything they could possibly do to avoid being together in the same room, it was difficult in a school the size of KCS where there was a common faculty room and lunch hour. Fortunately, Monday was Jimmy's turn at lunch duty so it meant they saw very little of each other during that time. There was one awkward moment in the faculty room first thing in the morning when, over coffee, Tim asked Jimmy how he got home on Friday night. Jimmy simply said that Phyllis let him borrow her car and let it go at that. Then Phyllis added to Jimmy's explanation by saying that "Yes", Jimmy had borrowed her car but brought it back on Saturday and then she drove him home. This drew so many stares and knowing glances from a couple of the teachers that it made her sorry she had not kept her mouth shut. Later, when they met as usual in the parking lot they decided they should cool things around school for a few days. That would last for less than twenty-four hours.

****

Tony had stopped at the Holiday Inn in Oneonta on his way to Snyder's Corners on Sunday night and booked a room. When the clerk tried to pin him down as to how long he planned to stay, Tony was evasive. Since it was late when he checked in, he decided to wait until Monday to go over to Snyder's Corners. When he headed down route 618 on Monday morning, Tony was not sure yet what is was he was looking for, how long it would take him to find it, or what he was going to do when he did. He did know that whenever he found who bumped Joey off, he was going to have to avenge it.

****

Moe spent all Monday tracking down the number thirty-one through forty green model Polaris owners he had left on his list. All machines were in either good shape or if dinged up, the owners had either a logical explanation or an alibi for the weekend in question meaning they could not have dumped the body out at Loomis Pond. This left only eleven owners to go, one of which, Moe noticed, was Dr. Everett Shay, the Chief School Officer out at Kaaterskill Central School. Moe figured he would get to him later on Tuesday evening since Shay would probably be at school all day.

****

Everett Shay received two calls on Monday afternoon. The first was from Bob's Collision Repair to tell him that his ATV was finished and he could pick it up anytime. The second, which came collect, was from Milt Meyers telling Everett that he felt better and asking Everett to come get him that evening. Everett decided he would rather have the ATV than his wayward English teacher so he told Milt that he would come for him on Tuesday. Milt said that was ok, he could use an extra night's rest anyway. Everett went in to Oneonta at three-thirty to bring his candy apple red ATV home, and spent the evening tuning it up.

Chapter 10

Tuesday started out about like Monday as far as Phyllis and Jimmy were concerned. On one of their chance meetings and finding themselves alone, they agreed to get together at Jimmy's for dinner. Since Phyllis had never been there, Jimmy slipped her a note with directions to his place as he walked past her room on his way to lunch. He felt like a school kid again; passing notes in class. They agreed to a five o clock meeting.

****

Tony's Tuesday breakfast was the second decent one he had had at the Holiday Inn. Once finished, he drove back over to Snyder's Corners. Like the previous day, he still did not know quite what he was looking for, but was sure that, once he found it, he would know it. He had spent Monday just aimlessly driving up and down Route 618, kind of getting the lay of the land. In less than thirty minutes he had seen pretty much the whole of Snyder's Corners. The school, which was just outside of town, was, after the bank, the most impressive building.

****

For a county seat, Snyder's Corners was a seedy shell of what it used to be before the area was abandoned by its major industry and the mass production of the automobile allowed the population to shop elsewhere. The downtown area was now about two-thirds empty storefronts, the shopkeepers having abandoned their stores when Wal-Mart opened over in Oneonta and undersold them. The owners of most of the buildings then converted the stores and the rooms above them into apartments that were rented out to low income, primarily welfare, families. This resulted in an actual increase in the downtown population and caused a lot more pedestrian traffic on the streets, day and night, than the few stores seemed to warrant.

The only businesses that remained were those which catered to customers who had an immediate need. This meant the Tavern, which was the only bar in town, a pharmacy, a liquor store, an insurance agency, the county Sheriff's office, a health clinic run by Doctor Condro and a funeral home—the fact that these places were in the same general area was ironic but coincidental. Additionally, there were a couple of luncheonettes and a pizza shop in the immediate vicinity of the county courthouse/office building that catered to the county's office personnel. Most did their best breakfast and lunch business when the county court was in session and/or the board of supervisors was meeting.

Aside from the county court house, built in 1872, the county office building, and the WPA-built U.S. Post Offices, (circa 1936), the biggest, best built, and most modern building in town housed the Palatine National Bank. This was an edifice, which covered a complete block and included the PNB Bank Corp headquarters, offices, and a huge parking lot plus a drive-though banking window. The construction of this complex was the result of the infusion of urban renewal funds and was in actuality owned by the city who leased it to the PNB Bank Corp for less per month than one of the four-room apartments in the storefronts across the street.

Started locally right after the Depression by a group of Snyder's Corner's citizens, the bank served the community well and made the founders rich by local standards. Once the children and grandchildren of the founders took over, however, the bank seemed outdated and was not providing the profit the heirs felt it should. They saw their only option as being to sell it to an expanding NYC-based conglomerate with off-shore headquarters that promised to upgrade and improve services. One of the conditions of the sale was the need to provide a new, updated facility at no cost to the buyer so, when the conglomerate threatened to pull out its latest acquisition, the city jumped in with the offer.

In reality, all the new version of PNB Bank Corp did was to make it easier for the local citizens to get into debt with credit cards and exotic personal loans while increasing the difficulty of obtaining large, long-term loans, which could have helped the local economy. As far as the service was concerned, it actually was worse. With a constant turnover in minimum wage tellers and vice presidents-in-training, the local patrons and personnel became strangers to the bank's users. As a result, customers often needed to show identification in order to cash a personal check drawn on their own accounts with the bank.

With no investment in the local economy, the only new commerce in town was the five antique shops that catered to those tourists who wandered though. The owners of these shops were able to make enough during the summer months to close after Christmas and spend the rest of winter in Florida. The last grocery store had closed long ago, unable to compete with the supermarkets in Oneonta, so if anyone needed essentials like milk, bread or lottery tickets, they had to go to the Stop 'N Go out on Route 618. Located next to Maggie's Truck Stop, a notorious diner and pick-up point, this convenience store also was the only gas station in area. This created a monopoly which allowed the owner to charge whatever the traffic would bear for his product.

****

Tony also had discovered that Charley had been right about there not being a decent Italian eating-place in town. The only thing resembling a kind of Italian cuisine was offered at the pizza shop, which was run by a family of Latinos. Tony stopped in the first day for a slice that seemed to have a salsa based sauce and, although he was not sure, Tony swore the cheese tasted like Monterey Jack. This led Tony, while filling up with gas at the Stop 'N Go, to ask the manager, who was working the counter, if there was a decent place to eat in the town. The manager recommended the Snyder's Corners Tavern for its hamburgers or Maggie's Truck Stop. Tony had had a burger at The Tavern on Monday; he figured he would try Maggie's tonight.

****

Moe started his Tuesday with coffee and donuts at Maggie's Truck Stop. Sitting at the counter, he shuffled through the remaining eleven releases, arranging them in an order that would make his trip the most efficient. He moved Everett Shay's to the bottom, figuring to get to that last.

****

Everett did not get away as soon as he had hoped, being held up by a call from the board president about a problem with getting tickets for himself and his wife for the following weekend's football game. By the time Everett dictated a memo to the athletic director ordering him to mail passes to all the board of education members that would allow them and their families gratis entry to school events, it was nearly noon. He went to the cafeteria to see what was for lunch and, deciding against the stew, grabbed a PB and J sandwich and a bottle of chocolate milk. He would eat and drink these while on the road. It was nearly twelve-thirty before he headed his pickup truck out onto Route 618 for Canandaigua.

****

Moe had finished up with the ten of the last eleven owners before three in the afternoon and swung around to Dr. Shay's house, getting there at just four-thirty. There was no one home. On a trailer parked in front of Shay's garage, sat a candy apple red ATV. Moe got out, walked over to it and looked it over. Moe recognized it as a Polaris Sportsman since he had seen a few in the past week, but the paint was obviously not a stock color. He should have immediately been suspicious but since the machine had obviously been set-up for competing in ATV runs, he just admired the paint job and thought no more about it. He went to the door and knocked. When there was no answer, he slipped his card into the crack of the door just above the latch. He had written the date on the back of the card along with a note that he would be back later that evening.

"Later" proved to be a lot later. He made the mistake of going back to the office only to find it in complete chaos. Apparently, the deer-rutting season has started in earnest. Two of the three deputies were out on car/deer accidents and the third one was at the office writing one up. No sooner had Moe walked into the office than a 911 call came through. Over on County Route 3 a tractor-trailer had collided with a car when it had swerved to miss a trio of deer. While, this time at least, there had been no fatalities, the truck, which had been carrying pulpwood, had overturned and spilled its full load on the highway. The only injury was to the trucker who was being serviced by a girl he had picked up in the parking lot at Maggie's. While the girl had had her head in the trucker's lap at the time of impact, she was apparently protected by the padded dash. However, the road would be have to be partially closed until there was a wrecker available that was big enough to move the rig out of the west-bound lane and a crew from the pulp mill got there to clear the logs off the road. With the other deputies tied up and since the accident was way across the county, it meant Moe was the only one available to direct traffic. He would also have to call in an ambulance to take the trucker into Doc Condro's clinic to be patched up.

At least it gave Moe a chance to run full out with his siren wailing. It would be well after seven by the time he returned to the office.

****

At the same time Moe was at his house, Everett was pulling in to the VA Hospital in Canandaigua. Milt was sitting on the curb with his bags all packed. He did not look bad at all.

As soon as Everett stopped, Milt jumped up from the curb and tossed his suitcase into the bed of the truck. When he opened the passenger side of the cab, a brown mailing envelop fell out onto the ground.

Picking it up, he asked. "What's this? Not those damn answer sheets, is it?" Milt held it up so Everett could see.

"Damn it, yes. Must be they slipped down between the seat and the door on the way to school a week ago Monday. I forgot they were there. Is there a note with them?"

"No note, just the package."

"Must be it blew out the window."

"Don't you think it's about time these got shredded?" Milt was curious rather than concerned.

"Yeah, tell you what, we'll stop at my office on the way by and I'll do it tonight."

"Ok. By the way, while I'm thinkin' about it. There are a couple of extra copies of those answer sheets in the bottom drawer of my desk, maybe I should go up to my room and get them too."

"You kept them? You idiot! They should have been destroyed long ago!" Sometimes Everett wasn't too sure about his old army buddy's thinking process. Of course, this was coming from the guy who had carried the incriminating answer sheets around in the front of his truck for over a week.

"No problem." Milt said, "We'll do them all at one time."

They spent the rest of the trip making small talk. Mostly about the army and the good times they had in Iraq. Everett told Milt about the buck rub he had found in the woods behind his house. By the time they got back to Snyder's Corners, it would be getting dark.

****

Jimmy's apartment was one of those over an abandoned store—an old hobby and train shop—just off Route 618. Phyllis parked around back and went up the stairs just at five o'clock.

The apartment was roomy, since it occupied the complete upper floor of the building. There was a full kitchen, living room, two bedrooms—one of which Jimmy had converted into an office—and a bath. It was much bigger than a single person needed, especially a bachelor, but the rent was cheap and Jimmy could easily afford it on his salary. When Phyllis entered, her first impression was how neat it was; definitely not her idea of the kind of place where a single man would live. Jokingly she accused him of straightening up to impress her.

"Not at all." He replied, his back to her. He was making spaghetti for dinner and was busily stirring the sauce. "My mother was a very neat person and she insisted her children follow in her footsteps. I always had to keep my room neat while I was growing up and it just stuck."

"Well, I like it." Phyllis said. Her mother had always told her that the best catch in a man was one who listened to his mother.

Phyllis walked across the kitchen and squeezed Jimmy from behind.

"Stop that, you'll make me burn the sauce. This is the world famous Kalid family, genuine Lebanese-Italian sauce. There is nothing like it in the world. If you want to do something, there's an open bottle of wine on the table, pour us each a glass." He pointed to the bottle and went back to stirring.

"Yes, my sheik." She gave a faux bow, touched her forehead like she remembered from some Middle Eastern movie and backed away. She filled the glasses that were on the table, and bringing one over to the stove, sat it within easy reaching distance of Jimmy.

"Well," he said, taking a sip, "how was your day?"

"Oh great. At least we're off the gothic stuff. In fact, we've completely switched genres. Today's film was *El Dorado*."

"O good, a John Wayne flick. Where does Meyers think that's gonna fit in? Well at least a good shoot 'em up should keep the kids interested for a couple of days."

"That's probably true but I won't be around for it."

Jimmy turned from the stove. "What?"

"Apparently Meyers' military exercises got over early. I got a notice from the office that he was coming back tomorrow and I won't be needed." Phyllis was not sure whether to feel bad or not. "I did get some good news though, when I stopped in the district office on the way out tonight, the secretary told me she thought there'd be something for me next week. Apparently there is a fifth grade teacher who is due to have a baby at any time."

"Sorry to hear you will be out of our building, I'm kinda getting used to seeing you around." Jimmy turned from the stove to see what kind of reaction that comment elicited. "But it's good that you'll have more work."

Smiling, she added. "Yeah, when the baby is born maybe she'll take maternity leave. It could mean a long-term sub job for me. Maybe even full time."

Suddenly Phyllis seemed preoccupied; there was a frown on her face. "Oh damn, I stopped to drop off the lesson plans and class roster book but forgot to leave the room key." She fished in the pocket of her skirt, drew out the key and laid it on the table.

"No problem, just give it to me and I'll take it in tomorrow."

Phyllis rose, went over to where Jimmy was standing and put the key in his front pants pocket—reaching in a bit deeper than was necessary.

"Knock it off." he was grinning. "Sauce is done. Let's eat."

Once seated at the table and more wine poured, they began to eat. Phyllis felt there needed to be some dinner conversation so she started. "Well, I told you about my day. How was yours?"

"Terrible", it was Jimmy's turn to frown. "I'm beginning to wonder what Meyers teaches the kids."

"What do you mean?"

"Well, most of the kids in my "regular" sections can't tell a noun from a verb, write a complete sentence, and, if they could, couldn't spell any word longer than four letters correctly. Not only that, but when it comes to simple vocabulary, most haven't gotten much beyond sixth grade."

"Maybe he's a lousy teacher." Phyllis twirled strands of spaghetti on her fork. Jimmy had been right, the sauce was wonderful.

"There are times I certainly wonder, what with him sitting his kids in front of a TV every period. I'm sure that doesn't stimulate them to think that much."

"Yeah, the old boob tube is not what they really need. He's training them to get all their news and opinions from either Dan Rather or Bill O'Reilly. "Phyllis was smiling. "There's certainly more to learning than watching images flash in front of your eyes—assuming you're awake enough to see them. Just what we need, another generation of zombies. I'm surprised he gets any kind of results."

"Me too, but, apparently it works for him. Hell, he's even gotten an award from the State Ed Department for his excellence in getting kids through the English Eight Comp Exam."

Phyllis looked up from where she was spinning some spaghetti on to her fork. "Is that a test given in June? Has a Part 1 answer sheet that includes some mark sense and short answer questions?"

"Yeah, that's it. The test's offered in January and June, but we don't semester and our kids always do so well we only give it in June. We don't actually use the mark sense part since Milt hand scores them. Why, did you see a copy?"

"Just last June's answer sheet. Meyers has a bunch of them in the lower drawer of his desk. The answers were all filled in though."

"You sure?"

"Of course I'm sure. There were five copies. One was an original, done in red ink, the other four were copies."

"That's strange." Jimmy stopped, a fork of spaghetti held in midair. "Wonder why he's got five copies?"

"Maybe so someone can help him correct the test?"

"That would make sense, expect he guards those tests with his life. A couple of times I offered to help him correct the Part 1 answers and he not only refused but got real defensive about it."

"Well, the answer sheets are there. I saw them myself last Friday." Phyllis did not think it was necessary to tell Jimmy why she was digging around in Milt's desk.

****

Tony was bored. He had driven around in circles so long and so often that the manager at the Stop 'N Go was getting suspicious. At one point, he had stopped along Route 618 where the path went in to Loomis Pond—he had asked at the Tavern the night before for directions—but, being a city boy through and through, he did not have the nerve to go into the woods. He had heard stories about there being bears and poisonous snakes in the area and was not taking any chances. Besides, he was sure, given his lack of woodsman's skills, he would not find anything anyway. Therefore, by six o'clock on Tuesday, he was not any closer to knowing who had killed his nephew than he had been when he left home. To make matters worse, he was hungry.

Pulling the Lincoln into the parking lot of Maggie's Truck Stop, he found a place between a couple of big rigs and parked. The tractors were running and, given the emptiness inside Maggie's, the drivers were either listening to their CB's , sleeping, or had some company in the sleeping quarters in the back of their cabs. To someone such as himself from the city, however, the diesel fumes were a breath of fresh air.

Entering the truck stop, Tony noticed there was only one customer. A short rather obese, man was sitting at the counter on the exact center stool. Tony took the stool at the end closest to the door and took the menu out from the holder by the napkins.

"Meat loaf's great." the customer offered. "This is my second one tonight. Nobody makes meat loaf like Maggie. I come in every Tuesday for it."

Tony regarded the stranger whom he now noted was wearing a sweatshirt, sweatpants, sneakers, and a lanyard around his neck that had a whistle and a large mass of keys hanging from it.

"Thanks, I'll consider it." Tony nodded.

A waitress appeared, placed a glass of water in front of Tony and assumed the universal waitress pose that, without a word being spoken, said "What are you having?"

Not being able to think of anything else, Tony ordered the meat loaf with mashed potatoes and peas.

"Good choice. Name's Mike Case." Mike got up from his stool, wiped his hands on his sweatpants and, walking over, offered the right one to the man on the other stool. "Nice ta meet ya. I'd guess you're not from around here if ya don't know 'bout Maggie's meat loaf."

"No I'm not." Tony, not knowing what else to do he shook the hand offered, wondering all the time how he was going to get rid of this mass of humanity that had just entered his space. "Just traveling through."

"Figered ya prob'ly some sorta salesman, judgin' from your suit and the car." Mike nodded with his head to the Lincoln sitting in the lot. "I coach basketball over at the Kaaterskill high school." He returned to his stool and began attacking what was left of the meatloaf, mixing it with catsup and the mashed potatoes on his plate.

At the name of the school, Tony's mind went into another gear. "That's right; I'm a salesman...school supplies."

"Kinda old fer a salesman though, ain't ya?" Mike gave the man at the end of the counter another once over. "Most of the guys I see sellin' stuff 'round school are a lot younger."

Tony's mind was now in fifth gear. "Well, I'm just substituting for one of our younger salesmen. Name of Joseph Scalani. This is his normal route but he disappeared a week or so ago with a bunch of orders." Tony figured maybe dropping the name would help.

"Sorry ta tell ya, friend, but that Scalani fella ain't gonna be runnin' his route no more. That's the name of the guy the sheriff pulled outa the woods a week ago Monday. Deader than a doornail."

"What?" Tony feigned surprise, "I hadn't heard that. Are you sure?"

"Yup, sure as shootin'. Shipped his carcass back to the Big Apple, last I heard. 'Parently he was from down there someplace." Mike was finished with his dinner and pushed the plate back. He was eying the pie selection. "Salesman, huh? Well guess that explains it."

"Explains what?"

"A couple of days before he came up missin' I saw him over by the school. Had a suit on just like you so I guess it makes sense that he was a salesman. He was lookin' for the CSO."

"The CSO?"

"Yup, Chief School Officer. The big honcho. Name's Dr. Everett Shay."

At last, Tony felt he was on to something. "Maybe I should go over to the school and see this Shay. If our salesman saw him, maybe he will have information on the missing orders we have with your school."

"Won't be able to do that now. I expect ole Doc Everett has gone home long ago."

"Does he live around here?"

"Yup, right down the road on Route 618, maybe 3or 4 miles."

""I wonder, could you be so kind as to give me directions to his house? If I can see Dr. Shay tonight, it'll save me stickin' 'round til tomorrow."

"No problem. Hell, I'll even draw ya a map." Mike reached for a napkin, took one of the waitress' pens lying on the counter and drew a detailed map. "Here ya go." he handed the map to Tony.

"Thanks a lot." Tony folded the napkin, put it in the breast pocket of his suit coat and started for the door.

"Hey", Mike called after him, "aint you gonna eat the meat loaf?"

"Help yourself" Tony was no longer hungry. He looked back in time to see Mike pull the just delivered meat loaf dinner over to himself.

****

After they had finished dinner and washed the dishes, they took their glasses of wine and adjourned to some lovemaking in the bedroom. While Jimmy was his usual self in bed, Phyllis noticed a bit of distraction when they finished. Sipping the last of her wine, she playfully asked. "What's up doc?"

Jimmy rolled over and sat up on the edge of the bed. "I've been thinking."

"Uh oh", Phyllis was still in a light mood. "Then it must not be you."

Through a smile he said. "Those answer sheets. What was Milt doing with them? Since the tests results had to be sent in to Albany back in June, he should have discarded them long ago."

"Maybe he just forgot. Not everyone is a neat as Jimmy Kalid."

"That's certainly possible. But why did he need four copies? This is getting curiouser and curiouser."

"Forget it. It probably doesn't affect you anyway. Want more wine?" Phyllis kicked off the covers, wrapped the top sheet around her waist, and started toward the kitchen for the bottle.

"But it might affect me. If Milt is pulling some sort of hanky panky on those tests, it may be affecting the background of the kids I'm getting in class. I've gotta have a look at those answer sheets." Jimmy got up, reached for his clothes, which were neatly folded on the chair next to the bed, and started getting dressed.

"Now?" Phyllis had stopped and turned.

"Why not? He'll be back tomorrow and then it might be too late. Besides, I have that spare key to his room so it won't be actual breaking and entering."

"How are you planning on getting into the school? I don't suppose you have a key for that too."

"Won't need one. Bill Case leaves the side door by the gym open so his kids can come in to practice basketball. I'll just use that."

"Well, then I'm going with you. For one thing I know exactly where the answer sheets are."

Quickly both Jimmy and Phyllis dressed and, since her car was closest, she drove.

Chapter 11

It was dark when Phyllis and Jimmy drove into the parking lot at the school. As Jimmy got out of the passenger side of the car, Phyllis reached around to the back seat and pulled out a six-volt flashlight.

"Better take this." she said, handing the light to Jimmy.

"Don't you have anything smaller?"

"Hey, it worked great on the lake back home. Besides, it's all I have."

The door, as Jimmy predicted, was unlocked. Jimmy listened carefully as they passed the gym and was glad to hear that there was no game going on. What he did not know was that after Milt walking in on him two weeks ago, Mike had stopped practice in case Milt turned him in. Mike figured he would wait a couple of days longer and if no one said anything, he would start again.

Milt's room was at the other end of the school. They had no problem negotiating the halls or stairs using the flashlight. Once at the door, Jimmy fished Milt's spare key out of his pocket and opened it.

"Jeez", Jimmy stopped as he entered and shone the light toward the front of the room. A large screen projection TV hooked to a DVD player dominated the front wall. It was so big that it completely obliterated the black board.

"Nothing but the best." chuckled Phyllis.

"I thought only the athletic department had a set up like that." Jimmy was examining the set closely "And they don't have a DVD player, just VHS."

"Over here.", Phyllis had gone to the desk and was leaning down to open it. By the time Jimmy got there with the light she had fished out the answer papers. "Here they are."

Jimmy held the sheets up to the light to examine them. Neither of them heard the door open.

****

Just as Phyllis and Jimmy were entered Milt's room, Everett and Milt pulled into the parking lot on the other side of the building.

Milt got out first. "I'll go up to my room and get those answer sheets. Meet ya in your office."

"Ok", Everett agreed, getting out and taking the envelope. Suddenly he stopped short. "Whoa! What's that?"

Everett used the corner of the envelope to point toward the window of Milt's room. There was a light moving around inside the room.

"Someone's in my room." Milt was stating the obvious. "Ya don't suppose they're after the answer sheets?"

"I don't know how anyone would know they were there or anythin' about 'em but, just in case, take this." Everett reached over to the gun rack in the back window of his truck and handed Milt the loaded, 12 gauge Ithaca Deer Slayer that he kept there for emergencies—like seeing a big buck along the road on the way to or from school.

Milt took the gun. Sprinting toward the front door with his key out, he unlocked it quickly and ran toward his room.

Everett took the envelope went around the corner and let himself in the school's back door.

Taking the stairs two at a time, Milt only slowed when he reached the second floor landing. Carefully and as quietly as possible, he worked his way down the hall to his room. He opened the door just in time to see Jimmy Kalid holding the answer sheets up in the light of a flash light. There was someone else, a woman whom Milt did not know, with him.

"What the hell do ya think you're doin'?" Milt shouted, leveling the gun at Kalid.

Jimmy and Phyllis turned together to see Milt, standing in the doorway holding a very big gun.

Jimmy found his voice first. "Well, good evening Milt. What do we have here? Looks like some answer sheets for last June's English Comp exam." He hoped he sounded calmer than he felt.

"What are ya doin' goin' through my stuff? Put the flashlight and the papers down on the desk and move away from 'em."

Jimmy did as Milt directed and backed away from the desk. Jimmy made a conscious effort to keep himself as much as possible between Phyllis and Milt's gun.

Milt walked across the room and picked up the flashlight and answer sheets in his left hand. Using his right he was still able to keep the shotgun aimed in the general direction of Jimmy and Phyllis.

Jimmy figured if he could get close enough he might be able to take the gun away from Milt since he was now holding it in one hand, but he did not want to take the chance of Phyllis getting hurt.

Ever the gentleman, he thought.

"Come with me." Milt signaled with the gun to the door.

With Phyllis and Jimmy marching in front of him, Milt directed them to Everett's office.

Everett was standing in front of the shredder, a puzzled look on his face, when Milt entered with his two captives. Everett's puzzled look got deeper.

"What the?" he managed to ask.

"Caught these two goin' through my desk. Apparently they found the answer sheets." Milt, having put the flashlight down, tossed the answer sheets on the top of the shredder.

Then, noticing the brown envelope in Everett's hand asked. "Haven't ya shredded those yet?"

"Can't figure out how to turn the thing on." Everett indicated the shredder. " It must be broken."

"Christ, you're a mechanic and ya can't get a machine to work?" Milt handed the shotgun to Everett. "Hold this on 'em and let me try." He went to the machine and after fiddling with it but not getting it to turn on, stepped back and kicked it. That did not work either. Turning to Jimmy and Phyllis he asked, "Either of ya know how these things work?"

Both shook their heads.

Actually Phyllis had had a shredder exactly like this one in her office in Minneapolis and knew precisely how it worked but was not about to tell either man. Besides, since it operated electrically, it had to be plugged in and from her vantage point, she could see the plug was partly out of the wall socket.

"What are we gonna do?" Milt was beginning to run out of options and his toes were now throbbing from kicking the shredder.

"Well, we can't leave either the answer papers or these two here. Let's take 'em to my place while we figure it out." Everett was the superior officer so he knew he was going to have to be the one to make the decisions.

This created a problem since all of them had to fit into Everett's pickup. As it was not an extended cab model, there was not room for all four of them in the front seat, especially when someone had to hold a gun on the other two. Everett, being in charge, came up with a solution. He took Jimmy in front with him and told Milt to get in the back with the gun and Phyllis.

"He's not going to try anything if he knows you're going to shoot his girl friend.", Everett had already figured out that relationship. He had also figured out, too, who Phyllis was since he remembered being in the district office the Monday she had come in to fill out her income tax withholding forms and get Milt's lesson plans and spare key.

It sounded like a plan to Milt, so using this seating arrangement; they drove to Everett's doublewide. By the time they got there, both riders in the back of the truck were half frozen—Milt especially so since he sat perched on his suit case the whole way.

Milt got down out of the back first and jumped around trying to get warm. This was hard to do while trying to keep the gun trained on either Phyllis or Jimmy. Fortunately for Milt, neither noticed nor, if they did, did they try to escape.

Jimmy helped Phyllis down from the bed of the truck. He could see that she was cold so as they walked up the steps into Shay's house he put his arm around her for both warmth and reassurance. She snuggled against him and shivered, not only from the cold but also from the uncertainty of what was going to happen. Jimmy, in spite of his growing dislike for the men holding them and deepening distain for their intelligence, found himself worried as well.

"Have a seat." Milt prodded Jimmy toward one of the stools by the counter. Jimmy sat on one while Phyllis took the stool next to him. Both turned to face their captors.

"Well, what now?" Jimmy was trying to keep an edge to his voice.

"Yeah, What now?" Milt repeated the question to Everett. Milt, after all, had always been the follower and had relied on others, in this case the one who was both his commanding officer and his administrator, to do his planning for him.

"The first thing we have to do is tie 'em up." Everett indicated Jimmy and Phyllis. "We can't be holding the gun on 'em all the while. Find something to tie 'em with." Everett reached out, took the gun from Milt, and aimed it in the general direction of Jimmy and Phyllis.

Milt looked around. There was not any rope in sight and he did not know Everett's house well enough to know where to look for any. Then he spied a stack of VHS tapes on the table in front of the TV. Walking over to the pile, he picked up the top one, *The Best of America's Home Videos, Volume 1*. Taking it out of its jacket, he said. "I can use this. Besides this is a terrible show."

Everett agreed. Milt unwound a length of video tape and, using his knock-off Swiss Army knife, cut, with some difficulty, one end of the tape from the spool. Then, cassette in hand, he walked back to Jimmy.

"Both of ya put your hands behind your back." He first tied up Jimmy. Unwinding the tape as he went, he wound it tightly around first Jimmy's wrist and then his waist so Jimmy's hands and arms were tightly secured to his body. Cutting the tape lose from the cassette, he took a second length and tied Jimmy's feet together at the ankles. He then did the same thing with Phyllis. Trussed up like this, they could not walk except with a slow shuffle nor could they use their hands, but were still able to sit on a stool. They sat back down and tried to make themselves as comfortable as possible. Jimmy's nose immediately began to itch and he could not do a thing about it.

"OK, what next?" Milt noticed that Everett had leaned the gun up against the frame of the front door.

"Give me a minute, will ya?"

****

In his capacity as an administrator, it was Everett's job to make decisions about such things as budget, scheduling, personnel, and, assuming he could not duck it, discipline. He usually rendered these decisions after careful consideration as to their consequences and after allowing as much time as possible to see if the problem did not resolve itself without help. Additionally, Everett's decisions always had a bailout clause so if he detected any kind of animosity from the board of education, parents, teachers, or students (in that order), he could reverse or negate his decision. This latter part always required more thought than the actual decision because it was harder to set up and, thus, slowed the process even more. This was the first time since the Gulf War, however, he had had to make a decision that was actually a life or death one and, since he was not used to being in this territory, he was taking it slowly. He was sure there was not going to be a bailout clause on this one.

Everett now resorted to his "step aside" mode. While he was not, by nature, a violent person, he did not have any compunction about eliminating problems that stood in his way. In truth, he was not a natural killer and, during his time in service, had never actually shot his M-16 at anything that could have shot back. It was only when deer hunting that he had ever intentionally killed another living being; something he rationalized by considering the killing to be a kind of public service that rid the area of traffic hazards. However, he was not; as he proved by his actions back in the Iraqi desert, against allowing problems to die on their own. Nor did it bother him if his actions resulted in the death of someone if it solved his problem as had happened at his trailer last week. The two cases that resulted in three people's deaths were easily rationalized away incidents of collateral damage rather than actually premeditated murder.

Additionally, Everett was also self-serving and selfish. If the information about how he had allowed Milt to alter the test scores ever got out, the scandal would cost him his job and, with it, a sizable amount of retirement money. While if he retired today, his pension, without a doubt, would have been enough to support him in a lavish lifestyle in New Mexico, it would not allow him to fulfill all of his dreams. Besides, he had already worked a sizable increase in his salary into the budget for the next two years and he wanted it. To realize this full benefit, he needed to keep going until he reached the official retirement age of fifty-five. That meant staying in education at KCS and out of jail. Therefore, the way he saw it Phyllis and Jimmy represented a roadblock to that dream and, nonviolent or not, he had to think of a way to eliminate them without implicating either he or Milt, thus jeopardizing his retirement. This, in his mind at least, sealed their fates.

****

"So,", Jimmy's voice broke Everett's line of thinking , "what did you guys do? Falsify the results of the English Comp?"

"We didn't falsify them; we just changed the kids' Part 1 answers." Milt was actually proud of their plan and his part in it. "Wasn't that easy either. I had to figure out how to answer Part 1 so it would give all the failing kids the same right answers and a high enough score so when I adjusted their Part 2 scores so they'd have enough points to pass. Do you know how hard that is?"

"I can only imagine." Jimmy said.

"If I gave them all perfect scores on Part 1, someone would have caught on so I had to make sure the answers were just good enough, but not perfect."

"And then you made copies of them." Phyllis had figured it out too.

"Exactly. Worked perfect too until some dickhead in Albany started making statistical comparisons."

"Ah, the guy Moses Barkman stepped on out by Loomis' Pond." The pieces were falling into place for Jimmy. He was beginning to realize too that if they killed the State Ed Department guy, his and Phyllis' chances might not be too good either.

"That was an accident!", Milt protested, "We were just going to scare him and dumb nuts over there hit him too hard with that paddle." Milt indicated first Everett and then pointed to the paddle on the wall of the kitchen.

"I've got an idea." Everett, after being cited by Milt, was back to the moment. "These two are a romantic item, right?"

Milt nodded in agreement since it seemed that way to him, too.

"She owns that old trailer that used to belong to Harrison that sits back in the woods on the other side of town." The ideas were forming so quickly in Everett's mind that there was a danger they would come out before he had thought them through. "What if we take 'em over there, tie 'em together on the bed and burn the place down? Those old trailers are always catching on fire—oil burners or water heaters exploding—that sort of thing happens all the time. Most times nobody gets out alive."

"Yeah," Milt was warming to the idea. "We could use some more of this video tape to tie 'em together so it would look like they were screwing when the fire started. The tape would burn away so it would look natural. Hey, we could use these answer sheets as tinder; kill two birds with one stone, so to speak." He was proud of himself for thinking of it.

"How about our clothes?" Jimmy was not trying to be helpful but he figured if they had to untie them to get their clothes off at least he might have a chance to overpower the one with the gun and Phyllis could get away.

Phyllis, in the meantime, was thinking: *The idiots don't realize that's an all-electric trailer, no boiler or furnace to explode. I wonder what they will do when they find that out?*

"That's right." Milt said, looking at Everett. "Guess we'll have to have 'em undress themselves when we get 'em over there." He smiled at the thought of seeing Phyllis naked.

"Good idea." Everett was surprised that Milt actually came up with one. "Ok, let's get goin'. You take them, the cassette and the answer sheets out to the truck while I go into the garage to get some gas to use to make sure the fire gets goin' good."

Yeah, Jimmy thought, *that will make it so it won't be the least bit suspicious.*

Then Jimmy had another question to ask. "Tell me, why didn't you simply destroy the answer sheets when you had the chance?"

"That was his job." Milt, who now had picked up the gun, cassette and papers, pointed at Everett. "Guess he got so busy with his ATV that he forgot."

"Naw, I didn't exactly forget. The note I wrote to myself. Musta fallen out of the truck when I checked that dog I hit on the way to school."

"Did it say 'Destroy these'?" Jimmy asked, remembering the misspelled note he found under the dead coyote.

Then Jimmy remembered. "*Grandfather says that the coyote will sometimes give a person clues to mysteries that have happened or will happen.*" *Could that have happened to me? Naw.*

"Yeah. How did you know?" Everett asked.

"I found it along Route 618. By the way, somebody spelled destroy wrong, it's DE-stroy, not DIS-troy. And it was a coyote, not a dog!"

"That was him, not me." Milt pointed to Everett.

Everett snapped on the yard light with the switch next to the door. As he started out, his foot kicked a card lying just inside on the threshold. He stooped and picked it up. "Holy Crap!"

"What?" Milt craned to see.

"It's the Sheriff's business card. Dated today, says he's coming back later." Everett was holding the card like it was covered with some vile substance.

"Later today?" Milt was still trying to let it sink in.

"Yeah, Idiot, today. We'd better get these two outa here in a hurry. I don't know what in hell he wants but it won't do any good if they're here when he shows up." Leaving the door open, Everett dashed to the garage.

"Out ya go." Milt waved the gun to get Jimmy and Phyllis up and motioned them out the door. They half hobbled, half hopped out the door and down the steps.

"Not the back of the truck again?" Phyllis whined.

"Sorry Babe, but this time I won't have to be with ya 'cause with ya both tied like that, there is no way you're goin' anywhere. Besides you'll have your love to keep ya warm." Then Milt thought for a minute and smiled at his cleverness. "You're gonna be plenty warm pretty soon anyway."

With Phyllis and Jimmy loaded in the bed of the truck, Milt opened the door to toss the cassette and answer sheets on the seat. As he did, a car turned into the driveway.

Milt's first thought was it was the Sheriff but before he could panic the car came inside the circle of light cast by the yard light and he could see it wasn't a patrol car but a Lincoln Continental.

****

Using Mike Case's directions, Tony had no problem finding Dr. Shay's house. He turned into the driveway and rolled to a stop in front of a pickup in such a way that the beams from the yard light were directly in his eyes. This was unfortunate for Tony, since it prevented him from seeing that there was a man holding the gun directly in front of him and two people sitting in the bed of the truck.

Tony opened the car door and, standing behind it, made a simple statement. "Dr. Everett Shay, I presume." He was shielding his eyes in an attempt to see the person standing by the truck. It looked to Tony like the man was holding a stick.

"Who wants ta know?" The reply came from the man and he apparently was not going to admit to anything at this point.

"I'm Anthony Torrelli and I have a couple of questions to ask you about Joseph Scalani."

"Don't know any Joseph Scalani. So I'd suggest ya get back in your car and get outta here." The man raised the stick to emphasize this point.

"He does too. In fact, he killed him." A second male voice came out of the glare from behind the man who had answered Tony. The best that Tony could figure, there must be someone in the truck. Moving slightly so the glare was not quite as bad, Tony now saw that what he thought was a stick in the man's hand was actually a shotgun and it was leveled at him.

Realizing that something was wrong and that he might just be in a bit of trouble, Tony took evasive action. Using the door as a shield, he dove back into the car and grabbed the .38 from under the car seat.

****

Considering that Milt was probably the only male in Palatine County over twelve years of age who did not deer hunt, what happened next should not have been a surprise.

The Ithaca Deer Slayer he was holding was built primarily for shooting rifled shotgun slugs at large game animals such as deer and bear, and as such, was one of the more accurately designed shotguns for this purpose. Although he was not familiar with the weapon, with his army training and using such a well-designed firearm, he should have been able to take down a target. So it was hard to believe that Milt not only missed the man behind the car door but the whole of the Lincoln Continental. The slug, in fact, lodged in a tree about thirty yards down the driveway.

Additionally that was the only shot he managed to get off.

Almost everyone who has ever hunted deer has, at one time or another, heard about or had a touch of, a malady know as "buck fever", which when it takes hold of even the most experienced deer hunter can cause some strange behaviors. It is not uncommon for hunters, when suffering from the most intense form of this affliction, to grab rolls of breath mints or lip balm out of their pockets and force them into the chamber of their firearms. In other cases, they have emptied their gun by shooting into the air or the ground. Or, as now happened to Milt, without firing another shot, he simply ejected every shell out of the magazine.

Just before the man in the car returned fire, Milt realized that his weapon was empty and, at the same time, a tremendous feeling of panic seized him. When the sound of the .38 shot came from the direction of the Lincoln Continental, all Milt could think of was that it was an armored vehicle round, his gasoline truck was under attack and he needed to get to cover. Dropping to the ground, he began digging into the gravel of the driveway, all the time sobbing uncontrollably. His sobbing was so loud, in fact, that he did not hear the screaming coming from the direction of the Lincoln.

****

At the sound of the shotgun's blast, Jimmy, instinctively, and as best he could with his hands tied, pushed Phyllis down below the side of pickup's bed and covered her with his body. When the .38 went off and the screaming started, he tried to flatten them both further. He waited for a bit of time for the sound of the shots to die down before raising himself up to look over the edge of the truck's bed. What he saw by the yard light, was a fairly large man hopping up and down while holding on to the open door of the Lincoln Continental. At the same time, Jimmy heard sobbing coming from the ground in front of the truck. Pulling himself up so he has leaning over top of the pickup's cab roof, he located the source of the sobbing as being Milt, frantically trying to dig his way below the surface of the driveway using his bare hands. The Ithaca was lying off to the side, well out of reach and, since its magazine was empty anyway, useless. Jimmy helped Phyllis into a sitting position and then they both wriggled their way out the open rear gate of the truck to the ground.

****

Everett had been in the back of his garage looking for some rags to use with the gasoline when the car pulled into the driveway so he was not aware of its being there. However, he did hear the shotgun blast. Dropping the gasoline can, he ran out only to see a car, its door open and the muzzle flash of gunfire in the area of the front seat. Putting two and two together and getting six, he assumed the car to be the Sheriff's and that Milt and the sheriff or one of his deputies were in a fire fight. Not wanting to be a part of it, he looked around for a way of escape and immediately saw the ATV.

Hopping on, he started it up, backed off the trailer and headed through a second driveway that led from the back of the garage toward the road. He was not sure where he was going but he knew he wanted to get as far away from the shooting as possible, as fast as he could. Coming through the last of the trees, he hit Route 618, and gunning the motor to its highest speed, headed in the direction of the school.

****

A three-year old, ten-point buck, his hormones raging, was skirting the edge of Loomis Pond. Stopping to rub the last of the velvet off his antlers on a sumac, he picked up the scent of a doe in estrous. Aroused by this sensuous scent, he located her trail and crashed headlong through a large mass of brambles to follow her out the path leading from the pond's clearing toward Route 618. Like all bucks in his stage of rut, he thought of only one thing. He had to procreate as soon as possible with the closest female so that he could pass his DNA onto the next generation. Once this particular doe was impregnated, he would be free to go on to find another female that was just as willing. The more does the better but, given the short time the females were receptive, there was a certain frenzy about his activity. So he completely ignored his normal reclusive behavior or any discomfort from hunger or brambles and, if he encountered another male or anything that seemed to want to prevent his completion of the rut, he would fight it to the death.

The moment he reached the edge of the highway, he sensed that something was coming toward him from down the road. Stopping, he heard a loud buzzing sound and soon a light appeared, approaching at a high rate of speed. Fearing that this intruder might be some sort of challenge to his supremacy and, quite possibly was going to take the doe away from him, he turned to face the competition.

****

The factory intended maximum speed of a Polaris Sportsman is for between twenty-five and thirty miles per hour. Therefore the aim of its headlights, built into the front cowl, is such that it will provide illumination of objects at a safe distance in front of the vehicle traveling at, or near to, this maximum speed. However, Everett had modified his ATV so it could travel at faster than factory-designated speeds without having taken the precaution of adjusting the headlights to compensate for this. Since he usually did not drive it at night, this had never been a problem. Now, he was heading down Route 618 at a speed approaching seventy miles per hour, he was out-driving his factory-installed headlights by about half again their designed distance.

This was not Everett's only problem. Inasmuch as he was driving an off-road vehicle, the low-pressure balloon tires mounted on it were of the kind that would grip turf very well but would not do the same on the blacktop road. This meant when making rapid changes of direction on this paved surface, the deep treads and low pressure combined to cause the tires to fold over, rather than grip the road. Combining this with the limitations of the steering system, it made maneuvering the ATV mechanically impossible.

Therefore, by the time Everett saw the ten-point buck standing in the middle of the highway, its head lowered in a challenging position, it was too late to take evasive action, even if Everett had been able to.

****

A three-year old, ten-point buck in good health and in the early stages of the rut would have a live weight of from one hundred sixty to one hundred eighty pounds. Standing on a dry surface, all four legs locked and with its head down giving it a low center of gravity, that same buck was as solid as a bridge pillar. Hitting it at a speed of nearly seventy miles per hour meant there was not going to be a soft impact.

The first thing that happened was that all four legs of the deer, after holding just long enough to bring the ATV to a stop, broke almost simultaneously. Second, because the vehicle's speed went from seventy to zero almost instantaneously, it caused Everett Shay's momentum to carry him over the handlebars and impact on the part of the deer immediately in front of him, specifically the buck's head. Since the buck had lowered his head and Everett hit him head-on, the deer's spine compressed into a ridge column holding the head solid at the point of impact, this drove eight of the ten tines of the buck's antlers into Everett's chest before the spine snapped, killing the deer. Six of those eight tines hit vital organs. Dr. Everett Shay and the ten-point buck exited the gene pool within seconds of one another. The irony of the whole thing being that had Everett realized it, this would have been the biggest buck he had ever seen.

Chapter 12

The job of clearing County Route 3 was not finished until well after seven-thirty and Moe still had to write up the accident report on the pulp truck. He had offered to take the girl to wherever she wanted to go but she declined, saying that she would ride back in the wrecker. Moe noticed that the tow truck driver seem especially happy about that.

Back in town, Moe stopped in at Doc Condro's clinic to check on the trucker. Doc tried to be serious when he told Moe that it took only a few stitches to repair the trucker's major injury. Doc added that he thought the trucker would be ok in a couple of weeks but would be out of commission sexually for a while longer. Moe could tell that inside Doc was laughing his ass off.

Once finished with the paperwork and because it was getting late, Moe almost went directly home. He figured there was no way he could check an ATV for missing paint in the dark and he was tired.

Climbing into his cruiser Moe got to thinking. *If the only ATV Shay now owes is that candy apple red one I saw this afternoon, there is a good chance he's sold or swapped the green Sportsman he bought from Big Ed. These ATV guys are always trading their stuff at the drop of a hat, so you never know. But if this is the case, it'll mean I have another owner to track down and I'll want to be able to get an early start on that tomorrow.*

Maybe it was just that he wanted to get this part of the investigation finished or an unconscious, inner, cop thing but with this thought,

Moe reconsidered. So instead of going home, Moe turned the cruiser the other way on Route 618 and headed toward the Shay place.

He saw the ATV's lights before he saw the accident. Pulling off on to the shoulder, he took a quick look around and, seeing there was nothing he could do for the guy wrapped around the deer, he turned on the roof lights, got flares out of the trunk and began setting them up. That finished, he went back over to the edge of the road to get the signpost number off the green location marker. It was only then that he checked the victim. Using his foot, he rolled the body over so he could see the face and he recognized Dr. Everett Shay. The ID done, he went over to shut the motor off on the ATV. As he did, he noticed that the candy apple red paint on the front of the vehicle had been scraped off when it hit the deer. It was green underneath.

Maybe, he thought, *I've found my green, 2004 Polaris.*

Going back to the car, he called into the office. Deputy Pierce answered. Moe told him to send the ambulance out to sign post number forty-one on Route 618 and then come out to give him some help. "No rush though," he said, "it's a DOA. Also, on your way, stop at the clinic and pick up Doc Condro. We're going to need a coroner and he's going to enjoy the hell out of this one. It's really ugly."

He went back to the car and waited.

Fifteen minutes later the ambulance pulled up. Pierce pulled in right behind with Doc in the jump seat. Doc took one look at the man/deer combination and said, "I don't know about his family but if it were up to me I'd stick them both in the same coffin." Then he and the EMT's went about trying to figure which parts belonged to which victim. One EMT suggested calling in to the fire department for the "Jaws of Life" to cut the pieces apart.

Moe sent Pierce down the road to set a few more flares, and when he came back put him to work directing traffic around the accident. The EMT's had put up a tarp so the rubbernecks could not see them working on the body, but this only announced there had been a fatality, so people drove slower. Sitting in his cruiser trying to think of how he was going to word his report so some insurance company would not come down on him, Moe had that inner cop thought that, since he had missed the green undercoat on the Sportsman, maybe he missed more back at Shay's place. As soon as the ambulance had left and a rollup came out to haul the smashed ATV away, Moe sent Bill and Doc on their way (Doc thanked him for another interesting day) and finished his trip out to Shay's doublewide.

When he pulled into the lighted yard, he saw a combination of the damnedest things he had seen in a night of bazaar happenings. There was a man, curled up in a hole about six inches deep, scraping at the ground and crying uncontrollably. Sitting on the steps of Shay's doublewide was a couple, wrapped up in what appeared to be video tape, their hands tied behind their backs kissing in a pose like the one of the statues of the little Dutch boy and girl except they this couple had their tongues down each other's throats. In the front seat of a big-ass Lincoln Continental sat a man in a suit, bleeding from what appeared to be a bullet hole in the front of his right shoe. Moe was sorry he had sent Doc home.

Taking stock of the situation, Moe recognized the guy on the porch as Jimmy Kalid, a teacher over at the school, so figured he'd start there first. Taking out his trusty Swiss Army knife, he easily cut through the tape before he said a word. Finishing him, he did the same for the girl, whom he had seen around town but did not really know.

"Thanks Sheriff," Jimmy said, rubbing circulation back into his hands. "I was beginning to wonder how long before we were going to get out of this mess."

"You didn't seem like you were trying that hard when I came up." Moe said smiling and nodding toward the girl.

"We'll, we've had a rather trying evening." Phyllis put in. Her circulation was gradually returning as well.

"I want to hear about all of it but first we'd better take care of those two." Moe indicated Milt and Tony. "Know 'em?"

Jimmy began. "I don't know the guy in the car. Never saw him before, as a matter of fact, but he probably saved our lives. The guy in the hole, you may know. He's Milt Meyers, teaches English in the Junior High."

"And was about to take us to my house to burn us alive." Phyllis put in.

"Whoa." Moe put up his hand, "All in due time. But before you start, let me check the guy in the car. He doesn't look too good. Your little hole diggin' buddy looks like he'll probably stay were he is til we're ready to move him."

Moe, Phyllis and Jimmy walked over to the car where Tony sat, dazed, in the front seat. For some reason he had had the presence of mind to hide the gun under the seat but otherwise he had not moved since he shot himself in the foot.

"I'm Moe Mozeski, Sheriff of this county. Who might you be?"

"A-A-A-Anthony Torrelli" Tony managed to croak out his name. His voice had gone within thirty seconds of his beginning to scream when the .38 slug went through his foot and he realized what he had done. The scream, has anyone not being able to make it out, was a long drawn out "NOOOOOOOOOOOOOO NOOOOOOOOT AAAAAAAAAAAAGAIN!!" given at such force that it almost ripped out his vocal cords. "Cud I geta drink of water?", he croaked.

"Sure", Phyllis said and went into the doublewide to see what she could find.

By the time Phyllis had returned with a glass of water, Moe and Jimmy had heard Tony's story, at least as much as he wanted them to know. While the Moe used his first aid training to staunch the flow of blood on Tony's right foot. Tony related what had happened over the last day.

Giving the Sheriff his name, Tony said that he was an uncle to the late Joey Scalani and had been trying to find who had killed him. He had learned that the last place Joey had been seen alive was the school so had driven out to Shay's place to get some more information. As he got out of the car, the guy who was now lying on the ground, started shooting at him. He thought one of the bullets had hit him in the foot. Tony, wise in the ways of the mob, left out the fact that he had been armed

Tony had lost quite a bit of blood and, of course, the three toes from his right foot, but otherwise, once the bleeding was stopped, he would be ok. Moe and Jimmy helped Tony over to the front seat of Moe's car, got him seated and left him there. Moe figured once he got Jimmy's story he would run this wounded man into the clinic for Dr Condro to stitch up. *Doc isn't going to believe this either.* Moe thought. Moe did not ask further about how Tony got shot because he was really not that interested to know. He suspected though that it was probably self-inflicted, not from the shotgun.

Milt was another problem. Curled up in such a tight ball that it took both Jimmy and Moe to pick him up, one on each elbow, they had to literally screw Milt into the caged back seat of the cruiser. With Milt safely out of the way, Jimmy, Phyllis and Moe sat on the steps of the late Everett Shay's doublewide and Jimmy, with asides from Phyllis, told Moe everything he knew. He started with Milt's taking them hostage, and went through the point where Everett took off on the ATV. In between, they also filled Moe in on what they knew of the killing of Joey Scalani, including the fact that the paddle on the wall in the kitchen was the murder weapon. (Moe, of course, knew differently but did not say anything.) When they were finished, Moe told them that Everett was dead, having run into a deer out on the highway. He left out the gruesome details.

"Sounds like you two have had quite an evening." Moe said when they finished. "I'm afraid though, that it's going to last a bit longer. I don't have any way to get you to town unless you want to ride in the back with Meyers there. And I suspect you don't. So if you don't mind waiting, I'll call one of my deputies to come get you. At some point, someone will have to bring in the Lincoln too."

"That's ok Sheriff. Phyllis' car is at the school. It's only a couple of miles but we won't mind walking." Jimmy had answered for both. He knew he had done right thing because of the way Phyllis squeezed his arm.

"Ok, suit yourself." Moe got up, and after brushing off his uniform, he touched the edge of his hat in a two-fingered salute, and started to the car. "Good night then. I suspect I'll be talking to you once the DA gets all this sorted out."

"I'm in the book." Jimmy saluted back.

****

Phyllis and Jimmy walked down the shoulder of Route 618 like a couple of high school kids with their arms around each other's waists,. Once away from Shay's yard light, they both noticed for the first time that night that the moon was full. The moonlight made it easy to find their way along the road.

By the time they got to the accident site, there was not much to see, just a few flares burning themselves out and a big stain in the middle of the road. Phyllis shuddered at it, but they walked by without stopping. Too soon, they could see the mercury vapor lights in the parking lot at the school. Jimmy reached over and stopped Phyllis. As she looked up to him in the moonlight, he leaned down and kissed her.

He completely forgot he would have to chaperon a field hockey game the next night.

Some place, back in the woods in a clearing at the foot of Henrick Hudson Mountain, a coyote bayed at the moon. Three others answered it.

AFTERWORD

When **Milt Meyers** found out that Everett Shay was dead, he immediately calmed down and stopped hallucinating. With his partner out of the way, he had no problem rolling over on him and telling the DA every detail about the English-8 Competency Examination scam and the killing of Joey Scalani. Of course, he minimized his part and blamed everything on Everett.

Not that everything Milt offered was necessary for the DA to prosecute the case. There was enough blood and DNA evidence on the paddle, tarp and, after Milt told the police where to find it, the briefcase. However, since Milt had been cooperative, and to save the taxpayers of Palatine County the cost of a trial, the DA let Milt plead guilty to accessory to second-degree manslaughter. Milt elected to have a nonjury trial so, after a short deliberation, the county judge sentenced Milt to three to five years in state prison.

A second trial in state court resulted in the conviction of Milt on five counts of perjury, one for each year, for signing the proctoring affidavit stating that he had given no aid to the students taking the Competency Exams. The court sentenced him to serve one year on each count, this sentence to run concurrently with his other conviction. The State Education Department also rescinded his teaching award and his license.

During his second year in Auburn Prison, after achieving trustee status, the warden placed Milt in charge of the prison's educational division. Two years later, one of the inmates in the program was **Timmy**

Griffin who, when Milt berated him for being unable to conjugate a verb, attacked Milt with a shank carved out of a plastic spoon.   Milt bled to death before reaching the prison hospital.

****

The State Education Department opened a full-scale investigation of the administration of **Kaaterskill Central School** for failure to secure their English-8 Competency Examines properly and falsifying the results. Using evidence found by the Palatine County Sheriff at the home of the former CSO and based on testimony from one of the school's English teachers, KCS lost its accreditation and was taken over by the State Educational Department as a "failing" school. In addition, in order to prevent future manipulation of results, a new state testing policy was instituted which called for spot-checking by state monitors during testing days to make sure the exams were being administered correctly and the results were legitimate. To implement this new policy, the State Education Department had to hire two hundred new employees who were given the specific responsibility of making these surprise visits. Three of those hired were KCS graduates.

As far the results of KCS's competency exams were concerned, the Commissioner of Education appointed a special, blue ribbon panel to determine what should be done about the falsified student scores. After a year of three-day per month meetings in Albany, for which the appointee's expenses were fully reimbursed by the State of New York, the committee agreed that it would not be feasible to make the students retake the test and the scores should stand. As far as the State Ed Department was concerned, the problem was solved.

Not so with NYSPHSAA, Inc. Since this organization was made up by coaches and because they knew that a rule, by God, was a rule, they were not so lenient. The NYSPHSAA, Inc. conducted their own investigation, which concluded that since the students of KCS for the last five years had not passed all their Eighth Grade Competency Exams this made them academically ineligible to participate in interscholastic sports. This ruling immediately shut down the interscholastic athletic program at KCS for two years until the current crop of eighth graders and below would be old enough to compete.

There was one upside to the loss of the sports' program, however. Without the expense of coach's salaries, team uniforms, travel and game officials the school saved more than was lost from state aid and transportation costs. While the new CSO and some of the board members noticed this when they prepared the latest school budget, there was no way anyone would have suggested making this condition permanent. It did, however, prevent a huge increase in real estate taxes for the district during the two-year period.

One morning during that winter, a gray truck with U.S. Government license plates pulled into the KCS parking lot. Four men, wearing dark glasses, and dark blue suits, got out, went in to the Chief School Officer's office and removed the copy machine. Neither the secretaries nor the newly hired CSO attempted to stop the men.

****

None of the above had any effect on the careers of four of the five school board members who were easily reelected when their terms expired. This success had more to do with the fact that they ran unopposed than their ability to effectively lead a school system.

Only the fifth, the dairy farmer, left the board at the end of his term. He was able to lease his 500-acre farm to a natural gas driller for $1200 an acre so felt he could now return to farming fulltime. Given the falling price of milk and the increase in fuel and feed, he was able to farm for another dozen years before he was forced to declare bankruptcy.

****

Cindy and **William Jameson** pulled **James** and **John** out of KCS as soon as NYSPHSAA, Inc shut down the athletic program and enrolled them in Williams Academy, a private preparatory, educational institution, which prided itself on producing winning basketball teams. The other noted accomplishment of Williams Academy was that all its student-athletes went on to college with full athletic scholarships—assuming, that is, the student did not jump directly into the NBA or NFL. James and John, who, by the time they graduated from high school, were six-foot ten inches tall and had the ball handling skills of point guards, received scholarship offers from every Division 1-A college in the country. They spurned every one of these offers when, with their parents choosing to pay the tuition to Cindy's alma mater, they matriculated at Princeton where the twins fit in exceptionally well in the school's vaulted offense.

There, they led the Princeton Tigers to four consecutive Ivy League titles and NCAA tournament berths. The twins' best showing was in their senior year when a large, eastern school, which used a 2-3 zone against them, ousted Princeton in the National Semifinal. The twins picked that night to go a combined zero for thirty from behind the 3-point arc. After graduation and citing burnout, they broke the hearts of every general manager in the NBA by opting for graduate school; James for law, John for medicine, and never playing another organized basketball game.

****

Upon hearing of **Everett Shay**'s death, a woman, claiming to be his widow, came forth and sued, for a million dollars each, the Department of Environmental Conservation claiming their policy of deer management caused her husband's death; the Department of Transportation for failure to keep deer off its highways; and Polaris for faulty headlights and steering. The court threw out all three suits as having no merit. Specifically, the Polaris suit failed because Big Ed Graef had on file the release signed by Everett Shay.

The widow's total inheritance was the doublewide which she immediately sold to a nice couple of motorcycle enthusiasts from Philadelphia. Three months after they moved in, the doublewide exploded and burned to its axles. Senior Investigator **Sidney Boyce**, the BCI investigator at the scene, cited the presence of the chemicals used in the manufacture of methamphetamines as the probably cause of the explosion. No bodies were found.

****

Doc Condro stitched up **Tony Torrelli** and told him that he would recover just fine with the exception that he was now without the three toes on his right foot. Tony said that was ok, he was used to it. When the doctor recommended that Tony go a hospital for a few days to recover, Tony declined saying he felt he would get just as good care at the motel for a third less money. The sheriff dropped the Lincoln Continental off at the Holiday Inn the next day on his way to delivering Milt to the Otsego County jail. By Friday, Tony felt well enough to drive back to New York City.

While driving down the Thruway and as he was calling Clarissa to let her know he was on his way home, a state trooper spotted him talking on his cell phone and pulled him over. When the trooper saw the expired driver's license, he made Tony get out of the car and, searching it, found the .38 under the seat. Tony used his one phone call from jail to contact one of Grotto's lawyers, who advised him to plead guilty on the phone and license charges. However, the lawyer got the gun charge dismissed by casting suspicion on the car rental agency, saying his client had no idea the gun was there and one of their employees had obviously overlooked it from a previous rental. Since the supervisor from the rental agency had to drive upstate to answer the subpoena thus missing his weekly tryst with the returns check-in clerk, he fired **Juan Rodriquez** for causing the inconvenience.

Once home, Tony was so relieved to be free of the guilt over his nephew's death that he decided to set up a scholarship in Joey's memory at C.W. Post. Thus, the Joseph Anthony Scalani Educational Scholarship came into being, funded by his uncle who raised the vigorish on his loans by an extra one percent.

****

When it became know that **Joey Scalani** would not be returning to work because he was deceased and since he had no assistant to take his place, the Department of Testing and Evaluation was able to do away with his position and computerize it. This meant hiring a computer consulting company to write the software and devise the forms at a cost of three-fourths of a million dollars plus an additional five-hundred thousand for new computers. Also, since those in the Education Department did not trust the teachers to learn the new system by themselves, all teachers in the state had to be trained in the proper method of filing the new forms so as not to mess up the computers.

To correctly train personnel, the State Education Department instituted a series of Saturday workshops at various locations around the state whereby two "volunteers" from each school system would be trained in the new procedures. These trainees would, once the Ed Department determined they were proficient, go back to their respective districts and train the teachers there. Since neither the trainees nor their colleagues were paid for this training, the state saved several million dollars in implementing this new system.

****

Josh Fisher graduated from KCS and, using his grandfather's heritage, successfully applied for readmission as a member of the tribe. Taking the name Little Coyote, he moved onto the reservation and became involved in the tribe's governing council. Being both farsighted and an astute negotiator when dealing with the other members of the council and the legislators in Albany, he was able to push through the building of the casino. Josh was also responsible for the tribal slogan: "Gambling: more addictive to the white man than tobacco." This resulted in his becoming the casino's director as well as tribal treasurer.

In this latter position, he was able to use the profits from the casino to purchase land surrounding the reservation at top dollar thereby tripling the tribe's holdings and removing thousands of acres of real estate from the tax rolls. By building gas stations and tobacco outlets on this newly acquired land the tribe was able to sell these items tax-free and increase their profits while undercutting local, nontribal outlets

****

The following spring **Doctor Edward Condro** delivered a set of conjoined twins to a woman in Hendersonville whose common-law husband happened to be her first cousin. Doc told the reporter from the *Oneonta Star* that this was the fourth most interesting thing he had ever seen in his sixty-plus years of practicing medicine, all of which had happened within the last year. The residents of Palestine County got together in fundraisers and managed to raise $5000 for medical expenses so the twins could be separated. When a New York City hospital and surgeon did the operation gratis, the parents were delighted and invested the entire five grand in Lottery tickets at the Stop 'N Go. They won a total of $260.32.

****

With no basketball team to coach for the next two years, **Mike Case** spent his winters watching ESPN and making his weekly trek to Maggie's Truck Stop for the meat loaf. One Monday morning, during the fall semester of the third year, while pushing a rack of dodge balls out into the gym in preparation for his first period class, Mike suffered a massive coronary. When three students came in to tell him they had forgotten their gym shorts so they could not participate in PE that day, they found him slumped over the rack; head in the basket of balls. It was too late to revive him.

The school immediately closed for the day and the administration called in half a dozen grief counselors. The trauma was especially great for the male students, many of whom took the rest of the week off—that it happened to be the first week of deer season probably had something to do with deepening their grief.

Some parents, who remembered Mike's winning basketball teams, felt the school should honor the fallen coach in some way. Subsequently, with unanimous approval of the board of education, the KCS gymnasium was renamed the Mike Case Arena. There was a small, bronze plaque affixed over the door in his honor. Within six months, some student pried the plaque off the wall and sold it to buy a couple of joints from a trucker out at Maggie's.

****

Katie Lasher, her senior year of field hockey shortened, nonetheless managed a full athletic scholarship to play the sport at the University of New Hampshire. After graduation, Katie moved to Massachusetts where she married the assistant women's basketball coach with whom she had been secretly living since the middle of her junior year. When Iowa State University hired the UNH assistant to coach their women's team, she moved with Katie to Ames. Once Katie arrived there, she petitioned the University to start a women's field hockey program. Rather than start a new women's sport, which would have jeopardized the University's ability to finance their men's football and basketball programs, the Board of Regents voted to drop their Iowa State's championship men's wrestling program citing *Title IX of the Education Amendments of 1972* as the reason.

****

Moe Mozeski suffered from fallout resulting from the loss of the athletic program at KCS. The people in the county were so angered because he had been responsible for bringing to light some of the evidence which led to the closing down of the interscholastic program that they voted against him when he ran for reelection. **Bill Pierce**, who had an axe to grind with Moe for reducing him to part time status, ran against him as a Republican and won easily. Moe and Grace then sold their interest in the Snyder Milking Sheep Farm to the recently married Martha and retired to Miami. Once settled there, Moe opened a small, part-time, private detective agency.

****

When a large gas company discovered natural gas in the Marcellus shale under some of the property in Palatine County, the directors of the PNB Bank Corp immediately bought up huge areas for back taxes. This included the land owned by **Moses Barkman**. When the new sheriff and his deputies came to evict Moses from the bank's land, he threatened them with a shotgun and chased them off. This created a weeklong standoff that actually made the national television news. Eventually the confrontation was settled when Moses ran out of beer and was lured out by the promise of a case of his favorite brew. Due to the bad publicity, which led charges that the bank's directors may have used insider information to obtain the land and because he had no heirs, Moses was awarded title to the land for as long as he lived. At this point, the land would revert to the bank. He froze to death the following winter when his truck slid into a snow bank on the way to town.

****

The week after what became locally known as the "Incident", the school called **Phyllis Nielsen** to substitute for the fifth grade teacher. When, at the end of the school year, the teacher on maternity leave decided she wanted to be a fulltime mom and not return to teaching, the principal offered the job to Phyllis. She took it.

****

The board of education did not give **Jimmy Kalid** tenure at the end of the school year. The reason, as related to Jimmy by the new CSO, had nothing to do with his teaching ability but rather was due to the fact he had testified in the testing scandal. Since this testimony resulted in the shutting down of the athletic program, parents had put pressure on the board of education to get Jimmy out of the district. The CSO expressed sympathy and, as way of apology, gave Jimmy a glowing recommendation.

Jimmy used this recommendation to obtain a job teaching Advanced Placement English in Brighton, a Rochester, New York suburb. The job consisted of four classes of AP English per day and, because of the extra work involved, Jimmy had no outside duties or homeroom. After one year at the school Jimmy, bored with the lack of challenge, resigned and took a job teaching in a small, two-room school on a sea island off the coast of Georgia.

Jimmy and Phyllis kept their relationship alive by long distance for the year Jimmy was in Rochester. They took turns meeting on weekends and holidays, weather permitting, at either his apartment in Brighton or her mobile home in Snyder's Corners. During their Christmas break that year, Phyllis spent Christmas with Jimmy's family in Buffalo, after which, they went to her parent's home in New Ulm for New Years. Both got along fabulously with the other's family.

When he reached the school in Georgia, Jimmy found that the other teacher on the island had quit so she could return to graduate school. With the approval of the county superintendent, Jimmy called Phyllis and asked her if she would like the job. She jumped at the offer, immediately quit her job at KCS, grabbed her cat and Norah Jones CD's, locked her trailer and drove nonstop to Savannah where Jimmy met her. She arrived on the island just two days ahead of Hurricane Alphonso.

After spending three days riding out Alphonso in a concrete shelter, while listening to Norah Jones on a portable CD player until the batteries died and eating nothing but peanut butter sandwiches, Jimmy and Phyllis went back to the mainland. Finding a justice of the peace, they married, figuring that with everything they had been through and to end up without a scratch, must have meant that they were destined to be together.

****

A female **coyote** gingerly approached the weathered trailer sitting in a clearing in the woods. She searched for the smell of humans and, detecting none, nosed her way through a break in the trailer's skirting. It was warm and dry inside, a good place for a den. Making a bed of the leaves that had blown through the hole where she had entered; she lay down and whelped six pups.

Notes to the Reader

Minimum Competence is a novel, specifically, a work of pure fiction triggered by a newspaper article about a school principal being investigated for cooking standardized test scores. Thus, like all fiction, it is based on some fact, in this case on several lifetimes involved in the New York State Education system—mine, my wife's, both my parents and many colleagues. This gave me lots of characters and characteristics to draw from when portraying the people, places and situations in this novel. Like Palatine County, Snyder's Corners and Kaaterskill Central School, all places and people are composites reassembled in my imagination. Any but passing resemblance to real persons, places or events now or in the past is purely coincidental. In fact, if you know a place, teacher, administrator, student, state department or board of education member that fits any of these of those portrayed, the fault is yours not mine.

The regulations regarding teacher licensing and tenure used in this novel were real and the ones in place at the turn of the century. As with all educational regulations and mandates, they were not written in stone and there is a tendency for them to change. Whether it is a new governor, commission of education or just some employee in the department who has spare time to brainstorm between their morning coffee break and lunch, new policies are being implemented with a fair degree of regularity. For whatever reason, they tend to be like city buses—miss one and another will be another along in a minute—so the chances are good that there may well have been changes implemented in the interim. There is a pretty good possibility, however, that whatever the new ones are, they will make more sense to the person or persons who authored them than to those who will be expected to comply. One thing you can be sure of is that since they were formulated by someone above the everyday teacher level, the chances they were put in place to improve the education system or facilitate teaching were not the main consideration. More than likely they were to make someone in the upper level's job easier and/ or reduce heat from some person or group.

As far as testing in the schools is concerned, be aware there is no English-8 Competency Examination per se in New York State but the exam in this novel is strictly a figment of my imagination based on types of exams given in this state as well as others. While New York State tests students' competency with statewide examinations in English Language Arts—as well as Mathematics and Science—at the end of fourth, sixth, and eighth grades, these do not resemble the exam used here. Although the Regents system of testing was used to distribute these exams, in New York State, only high school students (9 – 12) are given Regents Exams in an ever-increasing number and combination of subjects. I am sure, however, that the Education Department safeguards the answer sheets much better than in the scenario used in this novel.

However, the history of and procedure used to administer these state-wide Regents exams is correct, at least as it was in place for the thirty-five years I taught through 1995. There is not, as far as I know, a "Joey Scalani" type position in the Testing and Evaluation Department but considering that the State Educational Building in Albany is multistoried and filled with a labyrinth of cubicles, one may well exist. The State Education Department does, however, collect and evaluate scores on all exams to determine the efficiency of the various districts and can, if these scores are consistently low, make moves to improve the situation. This is usually done by publicly pillorying the district through press releases until changes are made but the threat of Departmental take-over does exist.

As far as teachers offering to "help" students to do well on the exams, it does happen. Given the pressure some districts place on their teachers to produce good grades, the desire of teachers to see their students do well, and the public relations competition between schools for good press, I am sure, in fact, that it happens more often than is acknowledged to the general public. Most often this "help" is given during the examination whereby the teacher uses body language, a raised eyebrow or a verbal signal ("Did you really check all your answers?") to alert the student to a wrong answer. Sometimes the student is even astute enough to catch the signal and correct the mistake. Additionally, when correcting the exam, a teacher may "accidentally" miss a slightly wrong answer or give extra credit for a less than perfect subjective one—some teachers have simply been known to add wrong. While the individual disciplines within the State Education Department set guidelines for scoring, there is some latitude given and if a mistake is discovered during a random state reevaluation of the exam, the district always has the option of taking the local teacher's mark rather than the state's assessment. This is as long as the error does not include credit for wrong answers or bad arithmetic.

Incidents of wholesale cheating by a school or teacher may sometimes happen, as it did in the central New York school that triggered this novel, but, because of the security measures built into the program, are surprisingly rare. When they do occur it is rarer still for the public to hear about them as the teachers and/or administrators are dealt with internally. Often they are reassigned within the district or allowed to resign, usually with a good recommendations and no black mark on their records. The educational system is good at taking care of its own.

The research and information in regard to snowmobiles/ATV's has been done by personal observation and talking to a couple of mechanics who are involved in various meets. While the speed of these machines may be a bit exaggerated for dramatic purposes both in the novel and by those who work on them, the information is fairly accurate—so I am told.

The University of Minnesota fight song is correct as far as I can ascertain and part of the public domain. It has probably been sung in worse places and by drunker individuals.

And, oh yes, I have a dent in the rear quarter panel of my pickup where, one October night, after I stopped to let a ten-point buck cross the road, he reared back and attacked the truck. Not once, but he backed off and slammed into it a second time before shaking his head and stumbling off into the woods. Sex can make males do the damnedest things.

Jim Mortensen
Oxford New York
March, 2009